Afterward

Bristol Vaudrin

Afterward

Bristol Vaudrin

Tortoise Books
Chicago

Afterward, I broke open. I cried. I held him so tight I left nail marks in his skin. What were a few more marks now?

The EMTs ungently separated us, and, with the coordination of motions necessitated a thousand times, they deftly lifted Kyle from the malignity of our apartment floor to a gurney that could barely contain his tall frame. They secured him under a thin blanket pulled all the way up to his chin and rushed him out our door into the hallway, past building onlookers, toward a waiting elevator, shouting to me which hospital to meet him at.

Then I was there, by myself, panting, kneeling on the floor, staring at my still-connected phone nearby with the 911 operator trying to get my attention. I disconnected and a moment later listened to the sirens reverberating off the impenetrable glass apartment towers around us as the ambulance pulled away.

I stared straight ahead, so flooded with emotion that none could get out. I fingered one of the smooth buttons on the front of my jacket until it felt uneven, and realized I had loosened the thread holding it on. I looked down at the ruined thread, thinking about how much effort it would require to fix it later.

I raised my eyes from the thread to the unholy mess that surrounded me, and thought of the money we had to put down to get this place, the most we had ever had to come up with, what almost kept us from getting the apartment.

The wailing of the ambulance was farther away now, and I could hear the disquieted murmuring of our neighbors outside our still-open door.

I picked my keys up off the floor, gathered my phone and purse, smoothed down my skirt, and walked—unsteady, chin raised—out the door into the sea of rubberneckers, locking our apartment behind me.

I do not remember getting in the elevator or pressing *P* so it would sink me down to the level of my car. But that is where I found myself. I do not remember making my way out of the gray parking cavern, across the snowy streets filled with work day stragglers trying to get home, to the hospital. But there it was. It loomed into view ahead of me, and I did not know if I had come to it or it to me. I followed the burning red *Emergency* signs, as this undeniably was an emergency, right? Or had that moment passed? Then I just kept following—following signs, following instructions, following people. It was all I could do.

I answered endless questions from untouchable people in glass enclosures whose entire job was to guide people through this plane that existed outside our normal lives. Finally, when all the check-ins were completed and necessary information provided, I sat down to wait. I was in the emergency room waiting area, my face paralyzed in a thousand-yard-stare, as hours or years slipped by, surrounded by people stuck in the sucking mud of sickness and trauma.

I needed to call Kyle's mom.

Instead, I called my mom. Voicemail. I wanted the recording of her voice to come alive and talk to me. But

I forgot, it is Wednesday. Mom is on a plane to Italy with two of her friends: her dream trip. "Mom, something's happened. Give me a call when you can."

I lowered my hand to my lap, still holding the now-dark phone. I stared, mute, at an empty wall opposite me. A woman in dull blue scrubs appeared in the way of my stare, and I slowly raised my eyes to hers.

"Lauren?" she said.

I considered the question, then nodded.

"I'm Nurse Lindsay. You can come back now."

I nodded again, and followed her out of the waiting area through a set of double doors.

The doors opened into a large, antiseptic hallway, housing beds separated by nothing more than what looked like heavy sheets hanging from the ceiling, and I found it impossible to not look at the other patients as we went by. I wanted someone—patient or staff—to scold me for the intrusion, but no one had the energy.

I was so distracted watching a gray-looking man in a bed weakly calling for help that I almost ran into the nurse, who had stopped in front of me at the foot of a bed. I did not recognize that I was standing at the foot of Kyle's bed until the nurse said, "Here we are," and gestured at his sleeping figure.

I gasped slightly, as if I'd come upon him like this without warning. Maybe I had, but that moment was hours in the past now. Now the gasp only indicated a crack in the wall of composure I had been building.

The nurse swung a cheap, hard plastic chair up to the bed. "Go ahead and have a seat, but let him sleep if you can. The doctor will be in after he's had a chance to look at the X-rays." With that, she pulled a ceiling sheet near the foot of the bed partway closed, and left. She may have done it to create the illusion of privacy, but I knew we were now just part of the lineup for the other emergency room voyeurs.

I stood next to him and stared while he slept, inanimate, under the harsh judgment of the fluorescent lights. How could it be Kyle?

I studied him, hunting for something to betray the imposter, but it was Kyle's free range brown hair, his eyebrow divided by a scar from where a baseball caught him trying to steal second base when he was eleven, and another nearly undetectable scar on his lip from mountain biking the year we met. He had shown up that night four years ago for our planned dinner with a cold pack on his swollen face, still leaking blood. My roommates had fawned over him while I pouted about the ruined dinner I had spent all afternoon preparing. He just grinned that quirky smile of his and said he was starving. Watching him eat my dinner that night, despite what had to be withering pain (and what I realized after taking a bite was terrible food), had stoked a spark. That was not the last time Kyle would show up injured, grinning, and packing a great story. It was one of the keys to his magnetism. I smiled at the memory, and cried.

I pulled the chair closer and positioned it next to his chest, where he would be able to see me without contorting himself. Or at least, he could once he woke up.

Outside his tiny, curtained pseudo-room I could hear the staff talking about a bad date one of them had had. Their laughter here seemed like a flower growing in rubble—hopeful, misplaced?

I noticed the black dress shoes of someone standing on the other side of our half-wall who seemed to be working there, because they were not moving off like all the other shoes. I stared at them; they were worn but immaculate.

A loose strand of my dark brown hair fell into my peripheral vision, and I tucked it behind my ear to delay having to take care of it properly. I looked reflexively at my phone to see if I had missed anything, but there was nothing.

I looked at Kyle again. I briefly, selfishly, thought about waking him. I needed to know what happened, and for him to tell me everything would be all right.

Beneath the blanket, his chest rose and fell with percussive monotony. I watched it, transfixed, tears streaming freely now.

Then, a doctor with a clipboard appeared in the opening between the curtain walls. "Knock, knock," he said, stepping in. "Hi, I'm Dr. Moreno. Are you Lauren?"

"Yes." I stood up but looked away, smearing tears across my cheek in a failed attempt to wipe my face clean of giveaways.

"Great, have a seat." He gestured to my chair and pulled another chair up to face mine. We both sat.

"And what is your last name?"

"Delgado."

"D-E-L-G-A-D-O?"

"Yes."

"So, Spanish?" he said, as he wrote it on the clipboard paper.

"My father was from Mexico."

He continued ticking boxes and flipping pages on the clipboard. "Ah, I just spent some time down there volunteering in a village. Where is your father from?"

"I don't know. He died before I was born."

He looked up. "Oh, I'm sorry."

I smiled politely, accepting the obligatory sympathy.

"Is your mother also from Mexico?"

"No, New Hampshire."

The doctor chuckled. "That's a long way from Mexico."

I smiled weakly. It was. And growing up in one looking like the other had left me feeling like a citizen of neither. Because in the small, friendly college town where I grew up, there were only a few others like me, and none I saw regularly—not on the playground, not in class pictures. In the Thanksgiving play I was cast as a Wampanoag Indian. Again. And again. And again. Until finally I came home in tears and my mother called my third-grade teacher, Ms. Martin, to suggest someone else have a chance to experience the role. (I can still remember Ellie Thompson's anguish when she lost her role as Pilgrim and was recast in my place. "But my family came over on the Mayflower!" she wailed.)

My mom said we were helping to educate good people. But that was a job I had never asked for.

She also worked hard to explore my father's culture with me. Every year for *Día de los Muertos*, we painted our faces and dressed up as skeletons. My grandparents would play my father's cassette tapes and the three of us would dance around by candlelight while Mom was cooking. We would buy the local florist out of marigolds, eat sugar skulls, and set up an altar for my father. On it, below his picture, we would set Coca-Cola, his favorite (though as a kid I preferred apple cider), and the special foods Mom had made, including his favorite enchiladas. We would take a raft of pictures, mostly of me, and send them, along with a letter carefully translated by the high school Spanish teacher for some cash on the side, to his mother, my *abuela*. We never heard back from her, but every year we continued to send pictures and a letter.

I remember when I was four or five, after checking the mailbox every day for weeks, I asked, "Why doesn't *abuela* write back, Mommy?"

She stopped what she was doing and took my hands. "Well honey, your father grew up very poor out in the country, so she may not have the money for paper and pencils and postage. But that doesn't mean she doesn't enjoy receiving our letters and pictures."

I nodded, hearing but not fully understanding this new detail about the man who contributed half of my genetic material, with no sense of what it meant to be him.

Even after I went away to college, my mom would send me a care package to celebrate my father on that day, and ask me to send pictures she could print out to send to her. Despite her best efforts, I still wore that culture like a backpack, rather than feeling it in my veins. The majority-white people of New Hampshire were my people, even though I was always a side glance away from feeling they were not. I did not have to codeswitch, because no one had told me the code.

The doctor with the clipboard was saying something. "And you live with Kyle, is that right?"

"Yes."

He made a note.

"Is he your boyfriend?" he asked, without looking up.

"Yes." This was all information I had given before, but I was thankful to be asked questions I had the answers to.

"It's been a rough day for you, hasn't it?" Now he looked at me earnestly, and I tried to push down the brick that had just developed in my throat. I nodded and lowered my eyes, refusing to believe I was going to cry in front of this doctor, though fresh tears were already rallying.

The doctor put his hand on my arm, then reached for a box of tissue. "Here."

I pulled the top tissue to my face and met the doctor's eyes again, as if lack of moisture proved composure, as if my red eyes were not already blazing the banner "not composed."

The doctor continued, flipping through several pages on his clipboard and looking at Kyle. "We have him on something for the pain. He didn't break any bones, fortunately, but there is obviously some other trauma. We're going to be moving him to a room in the regular part of the hospital, so that'll be more comfortable than our little tents here." He paused to look at me and smile, then continued. "And, of course, we want to make sure he's doing okay before he leaves the hospital."

I nodded.

He paused, looking at his clipboard. "The EMTs said you didn't know how long he had been like that when you found him, is that correct?"

"Yes."

"Okay." He looked at the clipboard again, then rapped his pen against it and stood up. "Okay! Do you have any questions?"

I shook my head, lying.

"We'll get him set up in that room as soon as we can. Would you like to wait here with him?"

"Yes, if that's okay. I mean, I know I'm not actual family."

He smiled. "In here, it's whoever shows up."

I smiled.

"Someone will check back in with you in a bit." He laid his hand on my arm again, giving me a reassuring nod. "Take care."

"Thank you. I will."

I still needed to call Kyle's mom.

I still had not called by the time the staff came in and said they were ready to move Kyle to his room. I gathered my belongings while they prepared him. He opened his eyes a few times, but he looked confused and drug-addled, and he quickly fell back asleep.

I followed the two staff pushing his gurney down the hall and past new security doors, ever farther into the maze. We were accompanied by a uniformed security guard who helped open the automatic doors. Then we turned down a new hall, decorated with warm colors and brightly painted art on the walls. We stopped in front of a door across from a nursing station where a middle-aged woman with bright floral scrubs and one squeaking tennis shoe helped wheel Kyle into the room. She smiled broadly at Kyle and spoke with a sing-song voice, as if trying to convince a skeptical toddler about the deliciousness of broccoli. "Here we go!"

I started to follow them in when the woman stepped in front of me, pleasantly but firmly. "Hi, you must be Lauren?" Now her tone said, *you are an adult. Eat the broccoli because you know it is good for you.*

I nodded.

"I'm Yancey, and I'll be helping take care of Kyle."

I looked down at her nametag to make sure I had heard her name right. She saw me and laughed cheerfully. "I know, it's a pretty strange name."

I blushed. "Oh no...I just..."

She waved me off, saving me from suffering through false denials. "Don't worry about it. After forty-plus years, it's grown on me."

I let my relief show.

"We just need a few minutes to get Kyle settled in, and then we can let you come back in."

"Where should I—"

"Oh, I'm sorry, you came in the back door! There's a little waiting area on the other side of the nurse's station. There are a couple of vending machines there, too. And I'll come get you as soon as we're done."

"Thank you." And I headed off to wait yet again.

The waiting area was empty except for one older man wearing a cap. He looked like he was nodding off, and was equally in danger of losing his cap and of sliding out of his seat.

I sat, weightless, on the edge of a chair, staring at the phone in my hand, knowing I should call Kyle's mother and that there would be hell to pay for every minute I did not. Even though it would be two hours earlier there, I was sure they would already be in bed. I also knew there was no time difference in the world that would excuse me from making the call anyway.

Still, it was a lot to brace for. I knew she would try to make it my fault, just like how I was the reason Kyle had not wanted to move back to his home state. (Even though he had told them he was not moving back after college, years before I had even met him. Though in all fairness, I had made it clear I had no interest in moving there either.)

And there was that conversation I had with his mother the first time I met his parents, their eyebrows twitching with surprise at seeing the brown-skinned girl Kyle had brought home from the city. They had talked about marriage and grandchildren, while I had brought up partnership and overpopulation.

"Don't your parents want grandchildren?"

"My father died."

"Your mother then," she said, neatly sidestepping my red herring.

"She's never mentioned it."

"Never?"

"No."

Helene considered this for a moment. "Well, you are young, maybe you'll change your mind."

"Maybe."

"How did your father die, if you don't mind me asking?"

"In a construction accident, before I was born."

"How awful! Your poor mother!"

For all the times I had had this conversation, or something like it, I had never figured out how to do it well. How to give someone enough information without giving the idea that I or my mother were permanently wounded by it. She had never remarried, not out of some misplaced devotion to the remembrance of him, but because she felt she had everything she needed for a happy life.

Kyle's mom did not strike me as someone who was happy in life, so maybe her active involvement in her sons' lives was an attempt to be at least happy-adjacent. If only she could get them to do what she knew they should do...

Out of excuses, I breathed in deeply, steeled myself, and made the call.

It was Kyle's dad who answered what had to be one of the last remaining residential landline phones in the country.

"Hello?" I had clearly woken him.

"Hi, Chuck, it's Lauren."

"Lauren?"

"Kyle's Lauren."

"Yeah, what's wrong?"

I could hear Kyle's mother, Helene, breaking through the barriers of sleep and comforters in the background, saying, "What's wrong? Is Kyle okay?"

"Well, Kyle is in the hospital..."

"The hospital! What happened?" he asked, before Helene's voice came from background to foreground. "The hospital! Give me the phone!"

After moment of rustling, I could hear nails clicking on the handset. "Lauren, this is Helene!" As if there would be some other woman in bed with Kyle's dad. "What happened! Is Kyle all right?"

"He's going to be okay, but he did...injure himself in our apartment."

"Did he break something?" I could hear lights being turned on and doors opening and closing.

"No, nothing was broken, thankfully."

Then it was quiet. "Why didn't Kyle call?"

"Well...uh...he's in the hospital."

The rustling started up again. "I'm coming right now. What hospital is he in?"

"I don't think you need to come—"

"What hospital!" She would not be dissuaded, or delayed.

"Eastern Memorial."

"I'll be there soon." With that, she hung up.

I slid back into the chair and groaned.

It was not long before Yancey's squeaking shoe announced she was coming to let me into Kyle's new room.

The security guard was standing outside Kyle's open door, and for the first time, I realized the black dress shoes I had noticed from under the curtain in the emergency room belonged to him. I looked at Yancey as if she were handing out cards with the answers to life's questions, but instead of a card I got a sympathetic look. "He'll make sure Kyle stays safe."

I eyed the man suspiciously as we walked by. He stared straight ahead.

Yancey escorted me in to where Kyle was sitting, propped up, bleary-eyed but awake. He smiled; he looked drunk to me. He reached out and squeezed my hand, squeezing a tear out in the process. I beamed at him.

Yancey made a quick exit, saying, "I'll be right across the hall if you need anything. Let me know if you need a break and I'll come in to sit with him."

Wow, I thought, that is nice. Without thinking, I went to close the door after her, but the security guard's hand on the door stopped me.

"The door needs to stay open." he said, looking directly at me for the first time.

I felt like I was back in high school, trying to steal a private moment with a boy in my room. I turned back to look at Kyle, but he was falling asleep again, so I flashed the guard a quick smile of acquiescence and walked back over to Kyle.

I pulled a new chair up to take my place at Kyle's side. It was a chair with a cushion designed to make long hours of waiting more bearable. It would be quite the chair if it could really do that.

My eyes drifted around the room. There was a window with a view of the parking lot, a television mounted high on the wall across from Kyle's bed, a small sink, rolling cabinets that saved the administration from committing to any one layout, and a variety of plugs, connectors, equipment, and purpose-built containers on the walls. It screamed "sufficient" in a palette that ran the gamut from off-white to beige.

I stayed at my new post, wringing my hands, as Kyle drifted in and out of sleep. My red eyes were too swollen to fully open, but I kept glancing at my phone in case the call came in without ringing and I could only rely on seeing it. But nothing.

Please call please call please call.

I walked over to the sink and splashed cold water on my eyes like I was trying to baptize them into a new and better-looking life.

Sure enough, as soon as my face was dripping wet, my phone rang. I groped for a paper towel from the dispenser and smashed it to my face before snatching up the phone. "Mom?"

"Are you okay? What happened? We just landed in Italy."

Kyle's eyes fluttered open so I stepped out through the doorway, back to the shock of lurid hallway lights and the—I now noticed—*armed* guard. I motioned to Yancey behind the desk that I had to step out to take a phone call, and she nodded and replaced me in the room.

"Oh, Mom, thank God. It's Kyle..." I said, skittering to the far end of the hall. I unleashed the day's events like a torrent.

I could hear the shock. "Oh, Lauren. Oh, honey. That is just awful. I'm so sorry. How are you doing? Is Kyle's mom coming?"

"Yes, I called her as soon as we got to the hospital." Well, I called her, anyway.

"Do you want me to fly back?"

"No. There's nothing you could do here, and I know how much you've been looking forward to this trip..." My chin trembled, and I covered the microphone in case I made any sounds that made her doubt my sincerity.

Silence for a moment. Then she said, "I should fly back."

"Do not fly back."

"Are you sure?" Real skepticism.

"Of course. Points for offering!" I said, adding to my mother's mountain of earned "brownie points," as if she needed more.

"Okay." Another pause. "I'll call you later when we get to the villa." She paused, and I could hear her swallow. "Wait, no. Lauren, I think I should fly back. I hate to think of you there by yourself."

I wanted her to come, and there was no way I would let her come. "Don't be silly, you just got off a nine-hour flight and you have a whole trip planned. I'm fine. Kyle will be fine. There's nothing you could do here to help. I already feel better just talking to you."

"Okay," She was unconvinced. "Okay. But don't be surprised if I show up at the hospital."

"I will tell hospital security to not let you in."

It was the start of the banter that had always said, "I love you," or "I'm sorry," or whatever it was that needed to be said between us. I am sure no therapist would ever approve of our method, but it worked for us.

"I will already be 'in.'"

"Then they will escort you 'out.' How embarrassing would *that* be!"

A weak laugh. "Okay, keep me updated."

"I will, Mom. Thanks."

The call ended and the warmth faded, leaving me alien and alone in the hospital hallway. I walked back to Kyle's room.

To my surprise, Helene arrived just a few hours later, as if transported there by mere desire. She had flown in from his childhood home where they talked about the snow level in terms of feet, where most people went to the same church their grandparents did, and where almost no one looked like me. I marveled at the flight schedule that could connect two such disparate points so quickly.

I had been resting my hand on his, studying him, when I heard her franticness at the nurses' station. She declared herself to be Kyle's mother and demanded to know which room he was in.

I took a deep breath.

Helene burst through the doorway, her blonde graying hair untethered, eyes wild, drapey clothes fluttering behind her, and muffled a wail at the sight of Kyle. If she had suspicions that there was more to the story than what I was saying, they were confirmed now.

The tumult of her entrance startled him, and his eyes flew open before softening at the sight of his mom. She fell upon him, covering him in tears and kisses and questions she did not need answered. Kyle winced.

Yancey had followed Helene in and now gently pulled her back from the bed. "Let's give Kyle a bit more space, Mrs. Hansen."

Helene withdrew slightly with a sob.

Yancey squeaked around to the other side of Kyle's bed and started to straighten and re-tuck his blankets. "Kyle isn't talking much yet due to his injuries, but that will come back with time." Helene stared down at her son, who gazed back at her from the unfamiliar repose of the hospital bed. Her tears renewed afresh.

Helene turned to me. "What happened?"

Yancey put her hand on my shoulder. "Why don't you two talk in the hallway? I need a few minutes with Kyle anyway."

Helene nodded energetically, as if it had been her idea. She pushed me out the door into the hallway and past the disapproving guard, then pulled me back to her in an awkward, violent hug.

"Lauren," she whispered into my hair, "thank you. Thank you for being there for him."

It sounded so artlessly rehearsed and absurd that I was not sure how to respond. Then the thought struck me that I just hoped her nose was not running into my hair. I gave her a requisite squeeze, letting her fill in the intent behind it, then pulled away.

When I stood back, Helene was dabbing her face with a tissue she had conjured from who-knows-where. She turned to face me and the information I held. She breathed in deeply and said, "What happened?"

In fits and starts, I told her what I knew. Understandably, she both wanted and did not want to know. And whether it was the fact it was my second chance at telling the story, or that it was easier to hear it under the severity of the hospital lights than in the shimmering beauty of Italy's sun, she bore it.

At the end, she turned away from me and walked a few steps, shaking her head and sniffling into her used-up tissue. After a contemplative moment, she turned back toward me, inhaled deeply, and nodded, saying nothing.

Drained from the weight of all that had happened, we both deflated into chairs in the waiting area and stared into the middle distance.

I could see her in my periphery. She stared ahead, turning her wedding band. The band was so thin, worn down by so many years of marriage, I did not know how it did not just slip from her finger and reabsorb back into the earth's crust.

I swung my gaze to my own fidgeting hands. I looked down at my jacket and saw that the thread I had compromised earlier had liberated its button. I sighed at the additional responsibility of replacing it. I knew I would never do it.

A short time later, Yancey summoned us back to Kyle's room. As we were walking back behind Yancey, Helene looked at Yancey's foot with a furrowed brow.

"Is that your shoe squeaking?"

Yancy laughed good-naturedly. "Yep, I call them my 'squeakers.' You know, instead of sneakers?"

I chuckled.

Helene looked at me without a trace of humor, then said, "That must be annoying to listen to all day."

"Nope. I don't even hear it anymore."

Inside his room, Kyle was propped up, awake-ish, with the security guard looking on. Yancey thanked him, and he nodded and silently resumed his post outside the door. Helene watched him leave, then not really leave, with some confusion. Neither Yancey nor I felt the need to explain it to her, and she did not ask.

The rest of that first night was tough and unending. Helene would drape herself over Kyle like a blanket before being peeled back periodically by the beleaguered hospital staff.

Finally, someone suggested she find a chair. Helene snagged one from the next room and dragged it up to Kyle's bedside, trying to scoot it to a spot equal to my own on the opposite side. But she could not quite get there because of the equipment in the room. I watched as she sighed and tutted and kept trying to adjust the chair, knowing I should offer her mine or help her with hers, but not doing it. Adding to her frustration about the chair situation was that the staff would push her chair out of the way when they needed to get to Kyle, leaving it to her to move it back into place.

Kyle would wake up during these intrusions, but talking appeared to exacerbate the pain in his throat, so he mostly just laid there quietly, smiling weakly, seemingly oblivious to the maternal angst in the room.

At one point, the staff needed Kyle all to themselves and they asked Helene and me to leave for a few minutes, closing the door behind us. Pushed into the hall and faced with the prospect of talking to each other beyond the emergency that had necessitated it earlier, we both made our excuses.

"Lauren, I'm sorry, I just want to call Kyle's father and give him an update, so I'm going to go down here where I won't bother anyone."

"Of course. I need to make some calls too."

It was not a total lie. It was now early in the morning Thursday, and I was supposed to be at work in a few hours with the rest of the nameless hordes slogging through the "work week." I do not think the company intended for us to be nameless, but it was so big it had no choice. It shot employees at corporate goals like a seahorse spraying out offspring. I did not even have my own job, I assisted someone else in doing his. Ostensibly, it was my duty to work my way up and replace him in that job someday, but that looked like a lot of work I was not sure I wanted to do, and was not that interested in.

It was late, or early, but I had to call my boss, Jim, to ask for some time off.

I dialed his number that I had in my phone but never called before, and after he answered, I awkwardly, formally, introduced myself, as if he would have trouble understanding who I was. "This is Lauren. I work for you?"

I did not intend the last part to be a question.

"Yes, Lauren." It was clear from his tone this had better be worth the interruption. I daresay this would meet the minimum novelty requirements for an after-hours call.

"I've, uh, had a personal situation come up, and I need some time off."

My request was met with the reluctance of a father whose sixteen-year-old son just asked for the keys to his Porsche. He would normally have been right to cast me some side-eye for a request like this. I was not the most motivated employee.

I explained the situation.

And I kept explaining.

Everything just kept bubbling out of me, and I raced to the end to beat the tears that were coming. It was more than he needed to know, more than he wanted to know.

"Wow." I could hear his shock. "I am so sorry, Lauren. Yes, of course, you can take some time off. Is he going to be okay?"

He had already forgotten Kyle's name.

"Yes, but he's going to be in the hospital for a little while longer." I held my breath, then added. "Please don't tell anyone at work what happened."

"I won't. I have to tell H.R., but it won't go any further than that." Jim said. "Keep me updated and hang in there. I mean...take care. Sorry, Lauren."

I disconnected the phone.

It occurred to me I should also let Kyle's work know, um, something.

I scrolled through my contacts, coming out the other end surprised that I did not have any of his co-workers' numbers. I will just use Kyle's phone, I thought, then remembered it must still be back at the apartment, unrecoverable as far as I was concerned.

In the end, after exploring many branches of his company's phone tree, I could only leave an awkward message at the end of a recording about job openings, in what I hoped was a human resources department voicemail box, saying that Kyle was at the hospital, injured, and promising he would follow up himself when he could.

I meandered back toward Kyle's room. The calls had been quick and I could see the door to his room was still closed, though the ever-present guard was still there. Is that the same guard? Maybe it is a new one. No, there were the same spotless aged black dress shoes. I noticed he was subtly changing his weight from one foot to another now, and wondered why he would not get comfortable shoes like the rest of the hospital staff?

I was still staring at his shoes when I noticed his eyes flit over to me. I quickly pretended to look past him at something else on the floor. As if that was a thing.

The exhaustion was really starting to hit me. I chose a nearby wall to lean against while I waited for staff to clear out of Kyle's room.

I watched as other nurses settled a new patient into a room at the other end of the hall. That person did not have anyone with him, I noted. So, we were doing better than him. Nice.

This part of the hospital was quiet at this time of night, or morning, and I could hear the dramatic cadence of Helene talking down the hall, even though she was speaking quietly. It occurred to me how much was conveyed without words, but mostly I was just relieved she was talking at someone else for a change.

A few minutes later, the staff emerged. I reclaimed my seat next to Kyle, and Helene appeared from the hallway to re-engage in her battle for chair equality.

Kyle was already falling asleep again. That left his mother and me with a lot of potential face-to-face time. Instead, I turned on the television. Helene whirled her head around to make sure it did not disturb Kyle, but he was snoring softly.

About half an hour later, I was dozing when Helene stood and declared she was leaving.

"I guess I will head to my hotel." Then she looked at me and raised her eyebrows, expectant.

"Okay," I said. I was sleeping—if you can call it that—in my chair, and planned to stay there.

"Are you staying here?"

Was she afraid she had been too subtle?

"Yes."

Helene sniffed and puttered, but finally left. I heard her talking to Yancey at the nurse's station on her way out and knew I probably would not be able to sleep there again.

The next morning, which was unfortunately only a few hours later, his mom was back, bright and early. Too bright and too early, I thought as I stretched my limbs, stiff from the uncomfortable hours I had passed in the chair.

As Helene settled in, I expected her to raise the subject of what led up to Kyle being in the hospital. I could understand why she would not do it the first night—after all, just him being there was a lot to take—but I thought those questions could come at any time, so I braced for them. But the opportunities kept sliding by, unrealized.

About an hour after Helene arrived, around the time I would have been getting to work, I heard from two of the girls I worked with, Megan and Hannah.

U ok? Hung over? Megan messaged.

Jim said fam emerg WHAT HAPPENED?? Hannah's message came through practically simultaneously, and I pictured them both at work, madly typing on their phones next to each other, Megan's black hair and Hannah's blonde side by side, the yin and yang of office gossip.

They, too, were being trained to someday overthrow their managers, but different managers than mine, and doing even less interesting work. Hannah's job in human resources seemed to be about making sure our floor had all the latest announcements pinned to the bulletin board, and pushing through a lot of different paperwork mid-stream, with very little genuine interaction with anyone else at the company. Megan's day in logistics involved responding to her manager about a million different details relating to things moving around the world—way too much interaction.

Kyle's mom pursed her already-thin lips at the disruption, even though Kyle was awake and watching television.

I'm okay TTYL

Sleep it off came Megan's response.

I silenced my phone.

Later that day, I checked in to a tidy little one-story motel on the edge of the hospital's campus, partly for convenience, and partly because I could not will myself to return to our apartment. After what had happened, it may as well have been full of mutant organisms trying to survive a nuclear winter. I could not imagine that the sun still streamed into the kitchen each morning, or that the groceries I had walked in with could still be healthy to eat; they, too, had been touched by what had happened. The apartment now dwelled forever in darkness, an ulcer on the earth, stage to a scene forever scorched into my memory.

I could have stayed with friends, I guess, but the thought of telling that story and answering those questions was too much for me to imagine. Plus, the secret blame that surely would be leveled at me when all our friends knew what happened. Maybe we could get through this, act like it had not happened. No one had to know, right?

The motel had probably never been nice, but it did strike me as competent. There was plenty of parking plowed free of snow, the room looked clean, and I was sure if someone came around asking questions like in the 1950s detective shows, the deadpan front desk clerk would exercise complete discretion.

I had not brought anything with me from our apartment, so moving in was complete when I set my purse on the almost-level table just inside the door. I sat on the scratchy comforter swaddling the bed and looked around—one large picture window facing the parking lot, a queen bed, a small table with one chair, a television stand with a modest television perched atop it, neutral walls with multiple layers of not-quite-matching paint patchworking the most damage-prone areas, and a linoleum floor making only the minimum effort to appear to be wood. This is what my underdeveloped credit could get me.

I would need to go to the store to buy a few essentials. My head was starting to pound, and I realized I had not had caffeine yet.

It took another hour to get showered and caffeinated, and to find my way back to the right part of the hospital in a new set of mediocre clothes. I kicked myself for only buying one outfit, thereby dooming myself to a similarly unsatisfying shopping trip again the next day. I swept through the main area with a smile and wave to Yancey and the other nurses, and a wary head nod to the security guard, which he returned. Kyle's mom was in the room with him, smiling a smug greeting from her position in the better chair. I wondered if they had talked seriously while I was gone.

"There she is!" Helene said, as if I had gone AWOL instead of to shower and change. I smiled back. Kyle smiled at me.

There was a lot of smiling going on, but not all of it was honest.

I walked to Kyle and squeezed his hand and kissed him on the forehead. I sat in the lesser chair but never stopped looking at Kyle.

Helene coughed, or laughed, and said, "Oh, should I give you two a moment?"

I know she expected that to break up our little scene, but I did not want it to. I wanted a minute alone with him to talk. I smiled at her again. "If you want to take a break for a minute, I'm here now and I can stay with Kyle."

"Oh." She looked at Kyle, as if for confirmation that she should leave, and when no objection was forthcoming, grabbed her purse from her feet, held her head up, and walked out.

Only after her steps receded into the perpetual "sounds of a hospital" soundtrack did I turn back to Kyle. "I'm sorry I took so long. I checked into a motel near here and had to buy a change of clothes."

Kyle crumpled his brow and looked at me. "Why?" His voice was impossibly raspy, and he flinched as he spoke.

"Why did I buy them instead of getting some from the apartment? And why a motel?"

Even as I said it, I saw he realized why. Kyle dropped his gaze into his lap. We had to have this conversation, and now appeared to be the moment.

I bunched up a fistful of his blanket in my hand. "I don't want to go back there."

He nodded, head still down.

"I can't go back there. Please. Please, can we move out of there?"

He covered my hand with his and nodded again without looking up.

"Is that okay?" I bent down, trying to catch his gaze.

He looked up briefly and I could see the tears filling his eyes. I bent over his bed and wrapped my arms around as much of him as I could, and I felt his arms encircle me.

"Thank you." I stayed there until I felt him release me. I kissed him again on the side of his face, and in my head, I was already planning our move.

I was surprised at how dull it could feel to be in a hospital with an injured loved one. I would have thought the worry alone would have kept me up night and day, caring for him, but the truth is that the laborless and helpless frame of mind a hospital suffuses is wearying. Kyle was sleeping a lot and talking very little while he was healing. Even the brief but necessary follow-up call to his work exhausted him and rekindled the fire in his throat.

The next day, Friday, my still-silenced phone lit up with an incoming phone call. It was the management company for our building. I had hoped to avoid this call for a few more days.

The television was on and Kyle was mostly awake, staring at it while Helene worked a puzzle in a magazine. I waved my excuses to the room and darted out into the hall.

"Hello?" I hunched into the wall to dampen the sound of my voice.

"Is this Lauren Delgado?"

"Yes."

"Hi, this is Stephanie from CB Property Management."

"Hi, Stephanie."

"Hi. Hey, we heard from some of your neighbors that you had to call an ambulance the other day. Is everything okay?"

I considered the question, at first specifically, then generally as it related to topics I knew I would have to bring up in this conversation. I was also hotly aware I was standing in an echoey hospital hallway, and tried to force myself nose-first towards a corner to create some semblance of privacy. "Um, yes and no." I breathed in, and told her what had happened.

"I'm very sorry to hear that." I got the feeling she already knew.

"The other part of this is...I mean...I've been thinking about it, and I don't think we can keep living in that apartment."

"I see."

"Because it would just be a constant reminder..."

"We have another apartment available with a different floor plan? It's on a lower floor so it would also be a bit less rent than your current unit."

"I think we just need to make a complete change."

"Uh-huh." She was frosty now. "Well, legally you are responsible for all rent payments for the full term of the lease."

"I don't suppose there is an exception for a situation like this?" I said, hopefully.

Silence.

"Please..."

More silence, then "I would have to get that approved. I can submit a request..."

I exhaled a breath I did not know I was holding, and almost laughed with relief.

"*If* your request is approved, we would let you out of the lease, but you would forfeit your security deposit, and you would have thirty days to move out." I could hear her typing in the background. "I should add that there may be additional charges for things like cleaning or damages, if that's an issue."

"Okay." My voice was small.

"I say that because we have noticed an odor coming from your apartment."

"I'm sorry. I'll take care of it." Embarrassment scorched my cheeks.

"Thank you. If this is approved, we'll send you some paperwork to sign and return. It will also outline the charges and give your final move-out day. We'll also need your forwarding address."

"I don't have a new address yet...he's still in the hospital...but I will get that to you when I do."

A brief silence, then she said, "Thank you," then paused again. "I, um, just wanted to say I'm sorry about what happened, and I hope everything turns out all right."

I looked down at the cold tile floor. "Thank you."

I hung up and watched as my phone screen reset to a picture of Kyle and me from a few months earlier. We were cozied up in sweaters and hats on the street outside our then-new apartment with a background of brilliantly colored fall leaves on the trees that lined the sidewalk. There was only snow on that sidewalk now.

That afternoon, I made my excuses to Helene and Kyle and bee-lined for the privacy of the motel. I needed to make some calls I could not bear to make from the hospital. I sat in my motel room and went down a list of cleaning services.

I called the first number and drew a deep breath.

"Hi, we're moving out of our apartment and need to have it cleaned... Well no, it's a bit more than that, there was an emergency and I haven't been there in a few days and I dropped some groceries inside the door... Yes... Oh, you know, some vegetables, some frozen food... Um, and also..."

The real thing I needed cleaned was not an 'Um, and also' point. Rather, it was the main point. But my mouth just could not breathe life into those words. It was excruciating for me and for the person on the other end trying to grasp what, exactly, I was asking them to do. And for the next person at the next company. And the next one. And the next one. They were not interested in doing a job they could not understand for a woman who would not explain it.

What they did not realize is that I could not. Family? Doctors? Yes, fine. Maybe even friends, at some point. But I could not bring myself to expose the rawest center of my life to people I did not know, who did not know me, who did not know Kyle. I balked at the thought of continuing to expand the circle of people I had told the story to. I did not want to become the person they might one day refer to in shorthand as "the grocery lady," or worse.

Finally, as I struggled through the same conversation I had just had with four other companies, I could not hold the pieces together any more.

"I'm not sure I understand what you want us to clean? Is it just the area by the door?"

A sob broke out of me. My seams were starting to give. Please, just help me.

"What's that?" the man on the phone said.

I started crying. Full-throated crying: the air going in fought the air going out.

"Whoa, whoa...I'm sorry...are you okay?"

"I'm...I'm...sor...ry..." I could not get words out between sobs.

"Okay, okay...does your being upset have something to do with this job?"

I pushed out a "Yes."

"How about this? I'm sure we can help you with whatever this involves, okay? We are certified for a broad range of cleanups."

I was forcing air in and out of my body in short bursts, but I was listening.

"What if we go take a look and see what needs to be done, and we can go from there?"

"Y...y...yeah?"

"Yeah. That'll be no problem. Do you want to meet us there?"

"No!" My voice broke and the pressure of impending tears pushed my throat closed again.

"Okay, okay. What if we come pick up the keys to the apartment from you, and give you a call once we're there?"

"O...o...okay." Now I was hiccupping, but calmly.

"Okay. Okay. Let me get a credit card from you, and an address for where to pick up the key, and I can send someone out on Tuesday."

Still hiccupping. "I don't know the...address, but I'll be...at...Eastern Mem...Memorial Hospital."

"Oh, I'm sorry." He softened even more. "No problem. Do you want to meet us in front of the main entrance at 9 AM on Tuesday? The van will have our name on it."

"Yes, thank you." I gave him my credit card information.

"Don't worry, we'll take care of this."

"Thank you," I whispered, then hung up, and lay back on the bed to welcome the release of the pressure I had carried since before the call. Part of it, anyway. "Thank you," I said to the universe.

I lay there for a luxurious, relaxing moment, then I rolled my head to the side to look at the time. I sighed. I knew I needed to get back to the hospital. It had taken longer than I expected to find a cleaner.

I rushed back and had no sooner walked into Kyle's room when Hannah messaged me again, asking if everything was okay. I silenced my phone to head off Helene's sniffing disapproval. I responded yes, but that I would be out of the office for a while, and that I was busy and would tell her more later. I knew the "more" was really the point of her message. She prided herself on holding the power of being the unofficial news source in the office, but I was not excited about being the news.

During the first few days, there was a neverending stream of medical personnel coming in to see Kyle; I was thankful to have Yancey in the mix, switching out shifts with another younger nurse I got to know named Evie. I eventually looked forward to their interruptions as a break from the schedule of faceless doctor, Helene, television, faceless doctor, Helene, television, back to the motel to sleep, shower and change.

Yancey amazed me. She seemed unflappable in the face of a constant stream of neediness—from patients, from their loved ones, from doctors, from other nurses, and from hospital management. Everyone needed something from her. I was amazed she could keep it up, without complaint, day in and day out. I wondered if I could ever be that person at my job.

The next day, Saturday, I was sitting in Kyle's room with Helene when Megan messaged. *Sorry about your cat.*

I silenced my phone again. *What cat?*

Told Hannah your cat died so she'd stop obsessing about what's going on with you.

Ha.

Then a message from Hannah popped up. *Sorry about your cat.*

Megan continued. *She was not happy I found out first.*

I bet. She just texted me. How did you know she was going to say "Sorry about your cat"?

What else is there to say?

I nodded agreement, then went back to my duties as watcher of the healing.

Those were the days when the hours dragged by, when we knew Kyle would be okay, but he was apparently not okay enough to be released. Kyle filled his awake hours with television; Helene filled hers with a cheap book of puzzles she never seemed to tire of, and when I could not read any more of the mediocre book I bought from the gift store, I counted things: how many breaths Kyle would take in a minute, how many holes were in the ceiling tile over the television, how many hairs were on Kyle's forearm, and an abundance of other useless numbers. Helene caught me counting several times. I would be intently racking up numbers on some new project, and I would realize she was staring at me, bewildered. Whether it was my activity or me that bewildered her, I do not know. I just assumed she was thinking the worst and continued with my counting.

The next morning, I was absorbed in my phone, sitting quietly next to Kyle as he slept, when Helene burst into the room, holding a bunch of brightly colored balloons by their ribbons. "Good morning!" she sang. Kyle startled awake.

Helene went to his bedside and kissed him on the forehead. "Happy birthday!" she said, presenting him with a lollipop.

Argh. I had forgotten Kyle's birthday was today! I had bought him a record by an artist he liked, but it was hidden in the back of my closet in our apartment, useless for this moment.

Kyle chuckled and took the lollipop. Helene tied the balloons to the rail of Kyle's hospital bed. As if Kyle was not already getting more attention than he would have ever wanted.

I knew Kyle would not care about forgetting his birthday, especially under the circumstances. But neither did I want to be sitting there with nothing while his mother took a balloon-festooned victory lap.

"I thought we could play a game today!" Helene produced a small, brightly colored box from her purse. "Do you remember this game?" she asked Kyle.

Kyle rolled his eyes and nodded, but it was not a game I had heard of.

"Kyle used to love this game when he was young!" Helene set to work freeing the game from its straitjacket of plastic wrap.

"It's really dumb," Kyle croaked to me.

"Oh, it is not," said Helene, waving him off. "Lauren, did you want to play?"

I had never heard a less inviting invitation.

"I'd love to," I said, unwilling to be sidelined.

"Okay, here we go." Helene passed out cards to the three of us, and provided me with the briefest of explanations on how to play. Kyle tried to add to it, but Helene insisted he not strain his voice. "It's very easy. We'll just play a few rounds and she'll figure it out."

But I did not. Not really. Every time I thought I had, some new rule was trotted out for the apparently "special" situation that had just occurred. It was a dumb game.

A very frustrating half hour later, while I was trying to come up with a way to excuse myself from the game, Kyle abruptly waved off another round and relaxed back into his pillows. He closed his eyes and was asleep almost immediately.

His mother and I both quietly watched him. It occurred to me how odd it was that someone looking at the three of us would use the same word for his mother's feelings in that moment as they would for mine, when I was pretty sure that none of us would want the three of us to be intertwined that way.

Still, there we all were—intertwined.

Helene noiselessly gathered up the pieces of the game and tucked them back in the box.

I looked at Kyle sleeping, remembering the first morning we woke up in our first apartment together and how exciting it was knowing we both belonged there and no one else did. We had stretched out our morning, lying in bed, running to the bathroom unclothed without worrying about roommates, and planning what we would put in the refrigerator, knowing our food would still be there when we wanted it and not have fallen victim to a lapse in self-control of someone else in the house. Even though we had already been together for over a year, it felt significant.

Helene interjected herself into my rainbow of memories with an intrusive wave in front of my face, and, to my dismay, mouthing that she was going to the restroom down the hall.

I sighed and nodded. I tried to get back to that morning in bed, but the hospital and Helene kept pushing themselves into the frame. I could not wait to be back in that bed for real with Kyle. Soon.

At this point, Kyle was well on his way to recovery. The next day, Monday, after Helene and I had been shooed out of the room so a doctor could check on Kyle, Yancey came to talk to us in the waiting area, shod in her usual squeakers.

"A bed has opened up, so Kyle is going to be transferred to another part of the hospital where he will not be allowed to have visitors."

I looked at Helene, confused, but she was listening intently to Yancey.

Yancey went on to explain why he was going there, why we could not see him, and what to expect during this time. She explained the authorities needed to satisfy themselves he would not try it again, though I did not know why they would be required to care about it.

"Kyle agreed to it, so that's good." It was clear from the way she said it that it would have happened whether he agreed to it or not.

"How long will he be there?" Helene asked.

"That's up to the doctors. And Kyle. Maybe a few weeks?"

I looked at Helene again, for no real reason other than to see if she knew how to react to this news.

"When will he be transferred?" she asked.

"Soon. The doctor is writing the order now." As if on Yancey's cue, the doctor walked out of Kyle's room, writing on a clipboard.

"Can we sit with him until then?" Helene seemed to be taking this sudden change of plans in uncharacteristic stride.

"Of course. You can go in now, and I'll let you know when we're ready for him."

We were both silent on the way back to Kyle's room. When we got there, Kyle was sitting up in bed.

Helene sat on the edge of his bed, facing him. "Yancey said you're going to be heading off to the next phase of your healing." It was as close as anyone had gotten to talking about what had happened with him, and I was a little awed.

Kyle hung his head.

Helene shook her head and chucked him under the chin. He raised his eyes to her, but kept his head down. When she spoke again, her voice was thick with emotion. "I love you so much."

I could hear him swallow and they both leaned in to hug each other. I had never seen her like this. I had never seen him like this. Watching felt like a violation. I elected to wait out in the hall to give them their privacy.

I inched toward the door without either of them noticing. Then, for some reason, when I was a couple of feet from the door, I leapt out into the hallway, startling the security guard, who yelped, which startled me because I forgot he was there, and I let out a short scream.

We now had the attention of everyone in the area—nurses, patients, staff, and definitely Kyle and Helene.

My cheeks flamed and I gave a weak wave and smile to indicate everything was okay, even though all indications were that hardly anything was okay right now.

The security guard straightened his uniform and resumed his prior stoicism. It occurred to me that all a "bad actor" would have to do to neutralize him is jump out at him from around a corner. He glanced at me after I thought this and I pretended to look past him again. Because it worked so well the last time.

I took a few steps so that I was out of earshot, but could still see into the room. I did not want miss any time with Kyle when it was my turn.

I peered back into the room and saw he and Helene were still talking deeply. I sighed and lingered where they could still see me through the doorway, giving them their time together, but not so out of sight that they would forget the clock was running out on goodbyes.

Five minutes later, I could still see them hugging and smiling. I edged back into the room.

Helene turned to me. "Thank you, Lauren."

I approached Kyle's bed and Helene stood up, putting her coat and gloves on. "I'm going to give you two some privacy." Yeah, that was not your idea. I just did that.

Helene leaned in and gave Kyle a kiss on the cheek, holding his face with her other hand. I guessed it was so he could not escape. "I love you. Remember what I said."

"I love you too, Mom," Kyle said in his hoarse, still-healing voice. He was smiling.

She picked up her purse. "Goodbye, Lauren."

What, no kiss?

"Goodbye, Helene." But she was already out the door.

I looked back at Kyle and he smiled at me.

"I'm going to miss you," he said with some effort.

"Me too."

He pulled me onto the bed next to him and curled his arm around me. We lay there, quiet and content, savoring a moment of normalcy. After a brief peace, I heard Yancey's squeakers approaching.

"All right, you two."

We both raised our heads up to look at her, not willing to move more than that until forced.

She smiled at us. "It's time."

We lay our heads back down, looking at each other.

"I'll call you when I can." He brushed the hair back from my face.

"Okay." I rolled off the bed and stuck the landing with a flourish. Kyle smiled. He knew I always joked when I was uncomfortable. It was true: I did not know how to say this goodbye. I looked at Kyle seriously and put my hand on his. "Shiv someone the first day so they know not to mess with you."

Kyle smiled and Yancey chuckled. "I would not recommend that. They grow the orderlies big over there," she said.

I grabbed my purse and bent over to give Kyle the briefest of goodbye kisses. "You had better not meet someone in there."

He laughed and winced, putting his hand to his throat.

"Although, that would be a great story for the grandkids, wouldn't it?" I added.

"All right, all right." Yancey helped Kyle sit up, then swung his bare legs off the bed.

A man in scrubs bedecked with badges walked in pushing a wheelchair, positioning it next to where Kyle was now standing. The security guard supervised from the doorway. Yancey guided Kyle into the chair, lowered the foot pedals for him, and stepped back. The man pushed Kyle toward the open door, followed by Yancey. The guard was leading the way down the hall. It was in the middle of this commotion that Kyle looked back at me and I waved a silent goodbye.

I followed his makeshift parade out of the room and watched as they disappeared past the same doors we had come through on that first day—four days and seven lifetimes ago.

I turned and walked slowly toward the exit. Then I took out my phone and called my mom.

To my great relief, Helene flew home the same day. Less to my liking was her promise to return as soon as he was released. Still, this gave me time to look for a new apartment for us.

I did not hear from Kyle that night, though I did hear from Stephanie that our request to be released from our lease was approved, so I counted the day overall as a win.

The next morning was Tuesday, so I was out in front of the hospital—despite the fact I no longer had any business there—at 9 AM when the cleaning company van scooted into the parking lot and pulled up beside me.

A man in clean overalls and a matching hat leaned out the window. "Lauren?"

I smiled and held out the keys. "Yes, thank you."

"No problem." He took the keys. "I'll call you in about half an hour after I see what we have."

"Thank you."

I went back to my motel room and waited: stomach tight. The cleaning technician called shortly after that, as promised. He said it would be no problem to get our apartment cleaned up. There was no permanent damage.

I practically chortled with glee when he told me what it would cost. He could have doubled it and I would have thought it was a bargain. I would have paid double just for the fact I had made it through this entire transaction without having to say or hear any real description of what we were talking about.

The apartment was one step closer to being behind us.

I had hoped to hear from Kyle that day since I had not heard from him the day before, but by Tuesday afternoon, he still had not called. I decided to go out for a happy hour drink with friends to take my mind off the loneliness of the motel room.

I called a sorority sister, Emma, who had been my first friend here in the city, but who I had not seen lately. She was sarcastic, but quick with a laugh and always up for some fun. We had hung out quite a bit when I had first moved here and I did not know that many people. She had grown up here, and had invited me to join her and her friends at a few things. That was how I became part of the same group. That was how I met Kyle.

"Heyyy, Lauren!"

"Hey! I was thinking today feels like happy hour."

"Oooh, good call. Yeah, it's been a while! What time do you get off work?"

Oh, right—work. "I'm pretty flexible today. What about you?"

"I could probably get out of here by 4:30." "Here" was her family's insurance business, where she drove a constant stream of paper to turn it into money. It would not have been her first choice for a career, I knew, but she could not beat the good living it afforded her, and the business would become hers when her parents retired. "Where do you want to meet?"

"How about margaritas at The Cantina?"

"Are you saying that because you want to support your people?"

I laughed, because I was supposed to.

"But yes!" she continued. "How about inviting a few others?"

"Fine by me. Just don't invite that girl Emma. Gawwwd, what a bore."

We both chuckled.

"Maybe you just don't understand her. What grade did you finish in school?"

"The one with the naps."

"Huh, no, that's as far as she got, too. Maybe she is just a bore."

We laughed and signed off, and I thought how nice it was to enjoy some lightness after the weight of the last week.

A couple of hours later, I was at The Cantina a little early to make sure we got a table, and, because, bored. The fantasy suggested by the brightly colored decor and lively horn music playing over the speakers was just the break I needed from my current life.

Getting table—how many? I texted Emma.

4, then, *Leaving now*.

"There will be four of us," I told the smiling Latina in a brightly-colored traditional Mexican skirt at the front counter. Did she smile that expansively at everyone, or did she see in me an unspoken sisterhood? I doubted she would feel that way if she knew me.

The woman led me to a table in front of the window, undoubtedly to encourage more business by showing that they had earned ours.

I shed my coat and scarf and scanned the menu to see which iteration of margarita sounded good, and saw that more people had started lining up. I was glad I had gotten there early.

Then I saw our friend Sara, and everyone else did, too, because Sara was a natural, startling beauty you seldom saw the likes of—blonde and shimmering, plump where you wanted to be plump and not anywhere else. It would have been easy to hate her but her beauty ran all the way through, and I think her kindness paved her way through life as much as her looks. Sara did a variety of things that depended on those looks—modeling, television—but she also was the first person I met who could truly take a compliment, accepting with a sincere, humble "Thaank you," with the sweet twang in her voice that pegged her forever as "not from around here." It was totally unlike the gibbering objections I threw out when someone tried to say something nice about me. Still, it was surreal to have a friend in our group who was a real working model. It did not seem like something that happened in real life, to real people.

She quickly spotted me and gave me her most generous smile and most understated wave as she made her way to the table.

"Hi!" she said, peeling off her jacket. "Margaritas on a Tuesday! We're so bad!" We hugged and sat, giggling.

A few minutes later, Emma and another friend named Ann joined us.

Ann was an original member of this group of friends; I was only a recent inductee who had joined through Emma and Kyle. She was quiet, thoughtful, and smart. I liked her as much as I knew her, though— I winced to admit—I would also forget about her for weeks at a time. I often wondered if she would have been part of this boisterous group if she had come around now, rather than in middle school when the group first started to coalesce. I guessed not.

"Awww, Emma," I groaned in fake dis- appointment. "I didn't know you'd be here."

"Yes, I have some interesting new updates about the insurance field to tell you all about," she said, deadpan, initiating hugs all around.

Now everyone groaned. All that was missing from the scene were the margaritas, and our waitress came quickly to rectify that.

For the next hour and a half, laughing with my friends, I could pretend life was just as it should be, that I had spent the day at work and would be going home to Kyle afterward, that I was wearing clothes I picked from my closet and would sleep on my pillow that night. It was an easy and welcome break to hang out with them like nothing was different, and I wished desperately it were true.

The reality did not hit me until we all hugged goodbye for the night, which was fortunate, because I would not have been able to hide my watery eyes if not for the darkness that had fallen on this short, cold day. My friends walked off to their own lives, rich with loved ones and pets and jobs that they had to be at in the morning, but not me. All I had was my motel room.

My plan was still to get past this without any of them finding out what had happened.

On Wednesday, mid-morning, I was checking my bank balance and how much room was left on my credit card when a blocked number flashed on the screen. Not thinking, I almost declined it. Then I realized that of course Kyle would be calling from a different phone than his. I pawed at the "answer" button, which caused my phone to slip from my hand and helicopter to the floor, still ringing. I pounced on it and—more carefully now—connected the call.

"Hello?"

"Hey," said the scratchy, unfamiliar voice on the other end.

"Kyle?" I just wanted to make sure.

"Yeah. But I don't have long."

I was excited. "How are you? What is it like there? What kinds of things do you do?"

"Talk. Listen."

"To each other?"

"Mostly doctors, but also in group."

"What kinds of things do you talk about?"

"How I'm feeling. What I'm thinking."

I paused. "Do you talk about me?"

"Not really."

I was not sure if I was disappointed or relieved. Both, I guessed.

"What's it like? Is it like a spa?"

"No. I guess it's quiet like a spa, but..."

"No one's trying to give you a massage, are they?"

"No," he chuckled, then added, "Well, hey, I have to go."

"Noooo!"

"Yeah."

"Just hurry up and come home."

"I'll try. Bye." And he hung up.

I stared at the screen, resentful that *that* would be my call.

But Kyle called again the next day, and the next. In fact, after that we talked every day on the ward's phone, but between his damaged voice, group meetings, and doctor appointments, as well as my loss of how to handle conversations with someone I knew so well, who I clearly did not know at all, the calls did not last long. I just needed him to come home.

In those first days after he was in the new ward, after so many stifling and unfulfilling days in the hospital with Kyle, I filled my hours with as much normalcy as I could cram in. Not just the Happy Hour

Emma had put together, but hanging out with friends for coffee and shopping and movies. When it was just us girls, no one asked where Kyle was. I was surprised how easy it was to pretend everything was okay.

But as much as I enjoyed it, my credit card did not, and the stress of my finances was building somewhere in the middle of my chest.

I still had not been back to our old apartment, which meant my credit cards were groaning from the charges I had been running up for the motel, clothes, and from all the pretending I was doing. I also had not been back to work, which was shortly going to be a problem, but one I thought future me could wrestle with.

The apartment hunting, what little I had done, had been tricky. The landlords were proactive about finding new tenants, whereas I had been dragging my feet about becoming one, so that meant that a lot of the apartments on the market were going to be available in weeks or months, not the days I needed it in. Also, I was not the only one looking, which meant that my foot-dragging lost me a great apartment with huge closets that I had looked forward to cluttering.

On the seventh day after he went in, Kyle had news.

"I'm going to be released next Monday. Can you pick me up?"

"Of course I will! That's so great!"

"I'll tell my mom, too." Yay.

"So the authorities are satisfied by this hastily-delivered mental well-being?"

He paused. "I guess." He paused again. "I've been working really hard."

"I'm sorry, I didn't mean—"

"I think it's been helpful."

"That's great! It really is. I'm really glad to hear that."

"Thank you."

For a moment neither of us said anything, before I threw in an "um" and at the same time, he said, "I need to go."

"Okay."

"They told me to tell you to be here at 9 AM."

"Okay."

"You'll meet with Dr. Ehrlich first. He's the doctor I've been talking to."

"Okay. Great." I needed to meet with Kyle's doctor?

"He's a nice guy. I think it's been really helpful."

"Yeah, you said—um. I look forward to meeting him."

"That's great!" Kyle sounded genuinely happy. "Okay, bye."

"Bye." I hung up, then sighed deeply.

On top of the anxiety I had about meeting Kyle's doctor, I now realized I had an inflexible date by which I would have to return to the scene—aka "our apartment"—or ask someone for help. The strength of my desire to not have to deal with it could have held back an ocean. I was so averse that for a brief, glorious moment I considered just abandoning everything, until financial reality laughed at me.

Mom was still in Italy. I paced the boundaries of my motel room, rehearsing what I wanted to say, then called her with my tale of woe.

"Honey, just ask your friends to help. They will understand."

She did not understand. "Calling friends" meant drop-kicking open the Pandora's Box in which all the dire imaginable results of this situation were currently contained. What would they think of Kyle? Of me? Would they blame me? After all, they have been his friends longer than they have been mine. I squirmed at the possibilities.

"Mom, could you hire someone for me? I'm not working right now, and..."

She sighed, though lovingly. "Hire who, Lauren? An apartment-finding, house-moving, interior designer?"

Yes, actually. That would be perfect.

"I will send you some money to help get into a new apartment, but I'm sorry, honey, you are going to have to handle the details yourself."

I sniffled, and she added, "You can do it."

We signed off and I fell backwards onto the bed, wanting this to be a cry-able offense, but knowing it was not. Mom was right. As always. I knew I was fortunate to have many friends I could call, but for some reason, ticking through my mental list, I could not do it. For each person I thought of, I came up with a reason to cross them off.

But I had to call someone. I had to make a choice. If only Kyle was here to help me. (Of course, if he was, I would not need to move.) I groaned from the weight of it all.

In the end, I called Sara to ask her and her boyfriend, Alexander, for help. Her upbringing was heavy on "appropriateness," unlike some others I could think of, and I hoped that meant she would not tell the others about our situation.

She was shocked at my news about Kyle.

"Oh, honey, that's just awful! When did it happen?"

I hesitated, remembering I had just met her for margaritas a few days ago. That could not look good for me.

"It just happened. To tell you the truth, I don't even know what day it is." That part, at least, was true.

"Oh, Lauren, I am just so sorry. Is there anything I can do to help?"

"That's kind of why I called."

Sara was quiet.

"I need to find a new apartment for us and move our things over by Monday when Kyle gets out of the hospital, but I just can't go back to the apartment again and see…" The blockade in my throat was back, and I was trying to sneak words past it. "I just can't."

No points for subtlety, but fortunately, Sara was too genteel to draw attention to my clodhopping manners.

"Oh, honey, no, of course not. What if we got some folks together this weekend to move your stuff over once you find a place you like?"

My stomach cratered. I had not considered that they would need to involve more of our friends, but of course they would. What did I think Sara was going to do, just throw the couch on her back and march on over? So much for my selection process. Maybe she would, at least, forestall any gossip.

"Thank you *so* much," I said.

"Of course. Does that give you enough time to find a place?"

"Yes, I'll find something by then." I had to.

I said I would let her know as soon as possible the address for our new apartment. After I hung up, I imagined Sara and Alexander's calls to our group of friends: they were not really calls for help to move a sofa, so much as a demand that they not be alone with the burden I had dropped on them. I covered my burning face with my hands and wished for a fast-forward button on my life. But no, I had to live every exquisite moment.

The next morning I woke up determined—I had four days to find a new apartment. I was ready to pound the pavement and, if that did not work, ready to settle.

The first day was demoralizing. I walked and called and met and toured the entire day without finding one apartment I liked. I did not realize there were so many ways to object to an apartment.

On day two, I forced myself to repeat day one's activities, knowing that if I did not, I would be taking Kyle home to the motel on Monday, or, worse yet, our apartment. The thought made me cold, and I pulled my scarf around me tighter and shoved my gloved hands into my coat pockets.

Apartment hunting with Kyle had been fun. We had explored every corner of the city and role-played every permutation of who and what we could be in each new apartment. At a certain point, I had wondered if the reason we were still looking was because we did not want to give up the sport of the search.

"Look how close we are to the parks!" Kyle said as we hopped off the train to view another new apartment.

"We could get dogs!" I said, trying to get oriented to which direction we should be walking, but failing. After a false start, Kyle turned me by my shoulders in the opposite direction, and we started toward the apartment for real.

"Big ones!" he said. "That will slobber everywhere!"

"Small ones," I corrected, "with healthy slobber control."

"Small ones! Tiny ones! Ones so small we forget they are in our pocket and run them through the wash!"

I laughed. "Not that small."

"Okay, slightly larger small dogs."

"Chihuahuas. Chi Chi and Cha Cha. We could get them little matching sweaters. Ooo! Ooo! And *we* could get sweaters that match theirs! Yes!"

"*I'm* fine with that, because that's the kind of confident guy I am. But won't their friends at the park make fun of them?"

"Their friends *are* pretty judgy."

Kyle nodded gravely. "The names will be key. How about Leopold and Beckett?"

"Too trust-fundy."

"Or is it just trust-fundy enough? We want them to get into a good school, don't we?"

"What about Howie and Milton?" I offered.

Kyle exhaled, faux-frustrated. "Lauren, are you *trying* to get them beat up on the playground? I feel like your heart isn't really in this."

"I just didn't realize how much work it would be to have dogs!"

"Yeah," he agreed. "Let's skip it. I don't want to pick up after them anyway."

"That's a deal-killer. As soon as I have to pick up after you, into a home you'll go!"

"Ditto," he agreed.

"Ooo, what about a cat?"

"A cat!"

And on and on it went.

But that was then, and this is now. This is nothing like that; now is nothing like then. I sighed deeply and trudged on across spottily icy sidewalks to the next address, alone.

That day I found an apartment I was very excited about, until the manager said it would not be ready to move into for at least a month—or so she said after sizing me up. I had lived in this skin long enough to know there was no use appealing to a part of her that did not exist, and moved on.

Later that day, I found two others I felt I could make work, if I had to, which eased the pressure I was feeling. But I was far from excited about them.

Mid-day on the third day, I found it.

The neighborhood was a mix of straight, tidy houses and bigger apartment buildings. People were out walking on the sidewalks and there were pockets of cute shops and restaurants.

The apartment was in a regal 120-year-old brick building with beautiful, ornate stone trim, and lush, manicured landscaping. A sign hanging from an elegant wrought iron bracket on the side of the building read *Kensington Apartments, Apartment to*

Let with a phone number. I called immediately, and a woman responded.

"Kensington Apartments, this is Jenn."

Please oh please oh please be the one. "Hi Jenn, my name is Lauren, and I'm looking for an apartment that would be available right away. I saw your sign."

She confirmed it was available soon. We chatted about the apartment and the terms, and she offered to let me see it if I was interested.

I was.

Jenn, a chubby, middle-aged woman with red cheeks, met me at the front door. I stomped the snow from my boots and she ushered me into a grand entryway clad entirely in marble. We walked up a beautiful wood stairway that wound up and around to the second floor. "We do have an elevator, but I love walking up these stairs. I feel like I'm in a movie." Jenn said with a smile.

"It is a really beautiful building," I agreed.

"It was originally a hotel. It was turned into apartments about twenty years ago, but they kept a lot of the original details and copied them in the new areas they built out. I was the third tenant and I've lived here the whole time. I started managing it about seven or eight years ago."

"Wow." I was getting very excited.

We continued up to the third floor, with Jenn a bit winded by the time we got there. "Whew. I live on the second floor, so that's more stairs than I usually get." She cackled at her admission and stopped in front of a door steps from the landing.

I watched, impatiently, as she fumbled through her keys, then slowly tried a couple of them in the lock.

I wanted to snatch them from her and throw open the door myself.

"Ah!" she said when one finally clicked open the lock. She pushed the door open and stepped back for me to enter.

I walked through into a bright, spacious main room with a dining room separated by glass garden doors, wood floors, and a series of windows that looked out over the landscaping I had admired from the street.

"It gets all the morning light. And it has a nice view of the old church up the street."

I walked around, entranced, taking pictures to show Kyle and my mom. Off the main room was a kitchen with classic built-ins.

"Why would a hotel room have a kitchen?" I said.

"The kitchens were added when they changed it to apartments. They made it look original, but it's not." She opened a cabinet door to reveal a dishwasher. "See? You wouldn't find that in a vintage kitchen. They also put in air conditioners, which is unusual to have in a building this old."

"Wow." I opened a few cabinets, looked in a few drawers, then checked out the bedroom and bathroom. Jenn followed me.

"The bedroom is original so it isn't that big, but it does have built-in closets that are pretty big for the time." She opened one and I nodded apparent agreement, though I was a bit disappointed at how small they were. But there were additional built-ins and drawers in the bedroom, so I thought between that and stealing some space from Kyle (who could have lived out of a shopping bag) it could work.

"The bathroom is nice. And it has doors to the main room and the bedroom."

I nodded and walked through the bedroom-bathroom-main room circuit with a smile.

"Will it be just you in the apartment?"

"No, I live with my boyfriend, Kyle."

"Great. But no pets?"

"No, no pets."

"Good, good. The wood floors are original, so we don't want them getting torn up or stained."

I walked around in a circle, eyes sparkling at the perfectness. "I love it. I would love to fill out an application."

"Sure, that's great. We'll need an application from Kyle, too."

"No problem." I was not sure how I was going to make that happen, but Kyle knew about it, so maybe I could just fill it out for him...

"Are you both working?"

"Yes."

"Any bad credit or rental history I should be aware of?"

"No."

"Ah, that's great. You should qualify easily."

"How long will it take to find out? And how soon could we move in?"

"I can turn the application around in a day, if all goes well. We're going to re-paint on Monday, so you could move in by Wednesday?"

I looked around at the walls. They looked lived-in, but not abused. "It looks fine in here to me. Would you consider not painting so we could move in on

Saturday? Our plans changed recently, so we need a place by this weekend."

"Oh, uhhh..." Jenn looked around. "I guess it doesn't look too bad. We could do that. If everything comes back positive."

"Thank you!"

Jenn and I exchanged paperwork, and she gave me a separate application for Kyle to fill out and get back to her. As I left, I looked forward to hearing from her by the end of the next day that we would be moving in the day after.

After I left the apartment, I tried calling my mother but it went to voicemail. I sent her the pictures I had taken with the description: "Our new apartment!" I started to send them to Kyle, too, but then I remembered his phone was still at our old apartment.

With no real way to share my excitement about the new apartment, I funneled my energy into walking around the area surrounding the building, filling in the pieces that would form my new life—my new coffee shop, my new grocery store, my new restaurants.

After what seemed like an appropriate amount of time to have "Kyle" fill out his application, I completed it and sent it to Jenn. I knew he would be okay with it.

I remembered I had not eaten yet today, so I decided to try out one of my new restaurants. When the polite waitress there said she knew the building I was talking about and welcomed me to the neighborhood, I finally got to gush to someone about the new apartment, which of course made the food taste even better. I tipped well to thank her for her tolerating my higher-than-normal level of patron enthusiasm, knowing it would also pay off on future visits to the restaurant, which I was sure would be one of our regulars.

I was walking the long way back to my car, thinking of calling Sara with the new address, when my phone rang. It was Jenn.

I almost dropped the phone in my hurry to answer it. "Hello?"

"Hi, is this Lauren?" She did not sound as happy as she did earlier.

"Yes. Is this Jenn?"

"Yes. I'm afraid we can't let you have the apartment."

My feet rooted me to the sidewalk, refusing to go on. "Is something wrong?"

"We contacted your previous landlord and they said you are in the process of breaking your lease with them."

"Yes, but we are paying all the fees!"

"Why didn't you disclose that?"

"I'm really sorry, I didn't realize that was bad if we paid all the penalties."

"It might not have been if you had disclosed it. I also called your employer. They said you've been on unpaid leave for the last couple of weeks and they're not sure when you will be back to work."

I deflated. I spotted a nearby bench and sat heavily on it, feeling its cold seep into my bones.

"Kyle's employer said the same thing, and when I tried to call Kyle to ask about that, it went straight to voicemail. I tried to call several times but it just kept going to voicemail."

My phone beeped, announcing another incoming call—my mother. I ignored it, but it made it hard to hear Jenn.

"I'm sorry, all of those things are related."

"I could have guessed that."

Another beep from my phone: a new voicemail.

"I understand this all looks bad, but everything will be back to normal soon, with both Kyle and I back to work."

Another beep: a new message. I was getting exasperated.

"And we have never broken a lease before. We are paying all the fees we owe for that and leaving the apartment in perfect condition. You can call our previous landlord, too."

"I'm sorry, even if all of that is true, the fact you didn't tell me about any of this...we can't rent to you."

"No, please! We can give you a larger deposit?"

"I'm sorry, best of luck finding a place." With that, she hung up. The time for appeals was over.

I stayed seated on the bench with my new voicemail and message and mourned the apartment.

I looked at the message. It was from my mom: *It's beautiful! Call when you can.* I dropped my head back and looked up at the monochrome gray sky for a minute, watching as the heat of my breath swirled up into oblivion against its backdrop.

Then I hung my head, looked at my phone, and sifted through the recent calls. I selected one and it rang.

"Hello?" A man answered.

"Hi, this is Lauren. I looked at your apartment yesterday?"

"Yes Lauren."

"I'd like to submit an application, if it's still available." I crumbled a little inside as I said it.

The next day, I stood in front of what was about to become our new building. I could not help but compare this tired, unadorned building to the Kensington. I sighed and walked up to the front door, the poorly cleared sidewalks crunching with snow under my boots. It was time to settle.

I met with the man who showed me the apartment two days earlier, and we exchanged money and keys in the lobby, as if I was paying for a fix instead of my new home. Afterward, I went to the apartment to remind myself what it looked like.

It was fine.

It had a short entry hall that led into the main room, with an authentically vintage, dishwasher-less pocket kitchen on one side and a bathroom and bedroom on the other. It had the same high ceilings and hardwood floors most of the vintage apartments had. It also had a bunch of worn built-ins buried in layers of paint that I half-heartedly snapped some pictures of to send to mom.

It was on the fourth floor, and that meant some of our windows looked out into the branches of the trees, instead of a view. But it was a good neighborhood, with a lot of college students and young professionals to keep it humming. I had to try to make the best of it, so I told myself the branches would help block some of the sun in the summer, since there was no central air conditioning.

I called Sara on the way back to my car to give her the address and make arrangements to get the apartment keys to her. She said they were all set to move us the next day.

So the word was out now. I pictured our friends on their phones with layers of calls beeping in to talk about "what happened to Kyle."

I drew a deep breath. "Thank you so much for doing all of this."

"I'm glad we could help. Say, would you like to come meet a few of us for a drink tonight? I can get the keys from you then, and it will help take your mind off things. It must be so hard for you right now, poor thing."

"I would *love* to meet you guys for a drink." It was true. As much as I dreaded thinking about our friends finding out about Kyle, now that it had happened, I wanted to be in the protected center of the group.

"Good. Why don't we try that new club on Ash Street—8 PM?"

"That sounds great. I'll see you there."

After I hung up, I headed back to the motel. We were not meeting for a few hours, so I made myself call Stephanie from the management company for our old apartment to let her know the final date we would be out. She, of course, reminded me of all the ways they had to keep as much of our money as possible, including the fact that we would still be paying for the full 30 days from our "last month's rent" deposit, regardless of the date we would be out. I did regret losing our security deposit, though it was to be expected, considering. But other than a little healthy avarice on their part, cutting ties with them had been easier than I expected. I guess everyone involved was looking for a change.

"Oh," she said before she hung up, "we did receive a call from the manager of a new apartment you applied for."

"Yes, she called me."

"She did not sound happy when we told her you were breaking your lease."

"No, I hadn't told her. I didn't realize it was bad if we were paying for everything."

"You should *always* disclose that," she said.

I rolled my eyes and hung up without comment.

I also heard from my boss, Jim.

"Hi, Jim," I answered when I saw his name light up my phone.

"Hi, Lauren. How are you doing?"

"Okay. Kyle gets out of the hospital on Monday."

"Oh, he's still in the hospital?"

"Yeah, but he's doing better every day."

"Good. Good. I was calling to see if you had a timeline for when you might be back, but it sounds like it's going to be a bit longer."

"If that's okay. I'm supposed to meet with his doctor on Monday when I pick him up, so I'll probably know more after that."

"Sure. Why don't you give me a call Monday or Tuesday and let me know."

"Okay. And thank you for holding my job for me."

"I'm glad we could do it. Life goes on, right? I mean...you know. Sorry, Lauren. I'll talk to you next week."

He hung up before I could say anything. Or I could not say anything before he hung up. I sighed heavily.

After that, I stretched my normally-forty-five-minute "getting ready" routine into a luxurious hour-and-a-half. That is, it would have been luxurious if the shower spit more than lukewarm water, the yellow lights did not flicker while I was trying to put on my makeup, and I had more to put on than the bargain-basement coordinates that had been getting me through the last two and a half weeks. I reminded myself that the real luxury would be minimizing my time in this motel room.

I paused, mid-makeup, eyes half-flamboyant, and lowered my hand holding the mascara wand. I remembered how when Kyle and I first got together, I had gone to extravagant lengths to avoid letting him see me without makeup, sneaking off to the bathroom before he woke up to re-apply, until one morning in the dim pre-dawn silence, when I was feeling for my purse on the side table, I felt his hand rubbing my arm.

"Don't go."

I turned back and kissed him, even as I did, feeling my purse and pulling it to me. "I'm just going to run to the bathroom."

He wrapped his long arms around me, holding me in the warm troposphere of his body, trapping my purse in the tangle. "You're going to put makeup on."

"Whaaat? No...!" It sounded lame even as it came out of my mouth.

He pulled me over on top of him, him laughing and me protesting. "You don't need it. You are breathtaking," he whispered, gently kissing my face. "I love waking up with you like this."

I blushed and objected, and he let me wriggle free to stand, exposed, with my truth and my purse in the half-light. But then he propped himself up on an elbow and reached for my hand.

"I'm sorry if I embarrassed you. Go ahead if you want to. But you don't need it."

But I needed an explanation. "You don't like how I do my makeup?" I pouted, dropping my purse on the floor and crossing my arms protectively.

"No, it looks great. I'm just saying you look beautiful with and without it."

"I can't be beautiful both ways."

"Of course you can."

"No, I have to be more beautiful one way."

He rolled to the edge of the bed and swung his legs over to sit in front of me as I stood over him, hotly aware of my nakedness. He took both of my hands in his and looked straight into my eyes. "You know that shirt I wore out last week that you said you really liked?" he asked.

I already knew I was being led down a path to prove my own wrongness, but I did not know how to stop it, and I was a bit curious how he was going to do it.

"You said I looked good that night...when we went out with the gang."

"Yeah, you did."

He held my hands together and kissed them. "I loved that night. You hung on my arm the whole time and I felt like the luckiest guy there."

I giggled, knowing we had much more beautiful friends there that night. I smiled at him, remembering, too, how proud I was to be seen with him, loving the rich smell of him.

"Well, do you think I look good now?" With that, he stood up, naked, without a trace of self-consciousness.

My heart jumped and I breathed heavily. "Yes."

He massaged my upper arms and leaned over to catch my eyes again, his thick with meaning. "I think you are beautiful right now, too."

"Oh, I see, you think a naked girl is beautiful. Who'd have thought?"

"No, I think you are beautiful." He paused. "Oh, wait ...you are naked!" Then he threw me, laughing, on the bed and bounced on after me, and the real kissing began.

Back in the motel room, I tingled with the memory of the rest of that morning. But under the flickering lights of the motel room, it seemed impossible that it had ever happened, that I was here, that Kyle was there. It was all impossible.

I sighed and finished applying my mascara.

After getting ready, I dawdled at the motel, drove slowly to the club, and waited for a really great parking space to help fill the time. A spot opened up right around the corner—close, but not right in front, where I would be self-conscious about my mediocre parallel parking skills. I parked (eventually), locked the car twice, checked my reflection in the window, and grimaced. I buttoned up my jacket, thinking the less anyone can see of my outfit, the better. I could not wait to have my closet back.

Walking up to the club, I caught a glance through the front window of Sara and a couple of other friends, Kelsey and Priya, occupying a primo table. I resisted the urge to wave my excitement. A glamorous girl like Sara—it figured they would give her a great seat.

Priya and I had never been the closest of friends, but I was glad to see her. I think we were both used to sticking out in these situations, so we had that in common, at least.

Kelsey was often wherever the party was, so I was not surprised to see her here tonight. For someone who had yet to hold down a "serious" job, I was envious of the seemingly bottomless supply of money and time her family afforded her, as I was sure I would never have both simultaneously.

In the curtained entrance, I could feel the music push rhythmically against my chest, as if it wanted me outside, rather than in. I told the expressionless doorman my friends were already here, and after a short quiz on what they looked like, and the usual scrutiny of my ID, he motioned me through. I checked my coat, then made my way over to the table and collected hugs with a level of solemnity that seemed appropriate for what they now knew. We sat back down and Sara pulled me over next to her. I dropped the keys to the new and old apartments into Sara's hand, and she leaned forward and hugged me again. She started to say something, but it was smothered by the music. Leaning in, she shouted into my ear, "Meet you Sunday at your new apartment to give you your keys back?"

I nodded agreement.

"Three?" She held up three fingers for supplemental clarity on the time.

I nodded again, and she smiled.

The server arrived to drop off their drinks and take my order, and I was demoralized to see that her outfit, even with work-enforced limitations, was better than mine.

I realized I was nervous. I did not know what to say. Fortunately, they did not seem to know either, and because it was too hard to keep fighting to communicate over the music, we gave up and let the it fill the void. Soon, Kelsey stood up and pulled us all to the dance floor, saving me.

We danced for a few songs, and when the music changed to something a bit less driving, we went back to our table for a rest and a drink.

As soon as we sat down, Kelsey leaned forward and looked straight at me. "So..."

Before she could make any progress on her thought, Sara intervened.

"Kelsey is going to Spain tomorrow morning!"

Kelsey looked at Sara and I could see Sara give her a look that was full of meaning. Sara continued on, talking to me. "So she won't be there this weekend, but we have plenty of help anyway."

Kelsey stopped, taken aback, still processing what was happening.

"How long will you be there, Kelse?" Sara was unwilling to let this go any way but her way, and I thanked her for it.

"Uuuggghhh!" Kelsey stood dramatically, thwarted, and danced back out to the floor. Priya looked down at her lap.

Sara reached over and laid her hand on mine. "I'm sorry."

I forced a weak smile.

"Might as well dance, right?" Sara stood again, waiting for Priya and me to join her, which we did, relieved to be freed. The dance floor did feel like the safest place to be.

An hour or so later, when the crowd had closed in and the music was louder than ever, Kelsey got our attention and yelled that some of our friends were going to another bar about seven blocks away. "Let's go meet them!"

Sara motioned for us to go back to our table so we would be out of the way of people dancing as we figured our next move.

"Come on!" Kelsey was revved up. "Let's go surprise them!"

Sara smoothed her hair and straightened her dress. "I can't go. I have to be up early for the move, and I want to be well-rested."

"Yeah, I have an early day too," Priya said, "I'm going to head home."

Sara put her hand on Kelsey's arm. "But you should go! It'll be fun!"

Kelsey looked at me. "Come on, Lauren. You don't have anything to do in the morning!"

"No. Thanks though."

"Come onnnnn." Kelsey grabbed my hand and pulled, as if this was her new plan on how to get me there. I pulled my hand back.

"No, I'm just not up for it." There was no way I was going to let her corner me somewhere else.

"You all suck," Kelsey pouted.

We finished our cocktails and made our way through the crowd to the coat check. While we were lined up, waiting, a well-dressed man walked up to Sara, leaned in to say something we could not hear, and offered her his card, holding it between the tips of two fingers. She smiled graciously and accepted it, then turned back to us.

He paused, as if waiting for her to turn back to him again, as if she did not already have a smart, handsome man at home, plus a list of others willing to take his place. Then he disappeared into the crowd.

"The manager," Sara explained to us. "In case we want to be on the guest list."

Priya and I smiled in wonderment at what it must be like to go through life as Sara. But going through life *with* Sara was also pretty good.

Kelsey's pouting deepened. "No one ever gives *me* VIP cards."

"Oh, it was for all of us. I was just the closest one."

Kelsey furrowed her brow suspiciously.

On the way out, Priya and I followed Kelsey and Sara. The previously poker-faced doorman nodded as he watched Sara walk by, and Priya and I smiled at each other again, knowing.

Leaving the humidity and heat of the club behind for the chilling February air was shocking, so we all quickly bundled up, said our goodbyes, and headed off in separate directions, except Sara, who walked in the same direction as me.

As we walked, Sara entwined her arm in mine. "Lauren, I'm so sorry about Kelsey. I didn't tell her, but I had asked Emma if she could come help with the move this weekend, and I think Emma assumed everyone knew and mentioned it to her. I *told* Kelsey to give you the night off from thinking about it. But you know her…"

"I do. It's okay. I assumed everyone was going to hear about it." Tears were forcing their way to the fore.

We reached the corner, and Sara paused to give me a last hug. "Let me know if there is anything else I can do for you. You will be okay."

It struck me that this was not the first time Sara was stuck making the unthinkable in life seem normal. I wondered who else she had sat with, and what had happened to them. Or maybe this was just how they raised them in the South.

The next day was Saturday, moving day. I did not hear from any of our friends, and I felt alone and angsty in the motel. A part of me felt like I was missing out on the fun of getting together with friends that day, but the other part of me smacked me in the back of the head for being a person who felt that way, considering the reason for their gathering.

I tried to sleep in as long as possible, but that only worked until about 9 o'clock.

I needed distractions. I needed my thoughts to be on things other than the only thing I could think about. I waited until 10 o'clock, when I was sure she would be awake, then, ignoring the sinking sensation in my stomach, I dialed my co-worker Megan.

A scratchy voice answered through layers of pillow and blanket. "Hullo?"

"Hey, this is Lauren. You still in bed?"

"Lauren...?" I could hear her roll over and check her clock. "Oh my god, it's practically the middle of the night! Why are you up this early on a Saturday?"

"I wanted to see what you were up to today."

"It's not day yet," Megan moaned. "I'll call you when I get up."

The call ended and I sighed, staring at the phone. I leaned back on the bed and turned on the television. I felt like all I was doing lately was waiting, and I was tired of it.

After a noncommittal preview of the seven channels the motel offered, I turned the television off and swung my feet down off the bed and into my shoes.

There was not much within walking distance of the motel other than the hospital, so I hopped on a bus to the shopping district. I puttered around the stores, regretting the paychecks I had been sacrificing for the time off. As time dragged on with no call from Megan, I considered going to a movie, but I did not want to miss her call, so I continued my aimless slog.

Eventually, I hooked up with the slow-moving Megan. She had also invited Hannah, who was vibrating with excitement to meet up on a weekend. Megan had no choice but to invite her, as I saw it. Hannah would have seen it as the ultimate betrayal if we met up without her.

I laughed when I saw Megan, grimacing behind sunglasses. "It looks like you had fun last night."

"It's possible I did. I'm sure someone will tell me about it."

Hannah wanted to shop, and Megan wanted some restorative time with minimal expectations, so we repeated a few of the stores I had already perused, then gave up on appearances and went for cocktails. Megan was reinvigorated by a caffeine cocktail, so we ordered a second round, then a third. Megan and I were content to let Hannah babble, saving us from the effort of drawing on our own low batteries.

After we wore out our welcome at the first place, we moved to another bar that would not have the same compunctions about how many drinks we were having. We did not know this bar, but there was always one of them around.

My prudent thriftiness was now in thrall to the siren call of my credit card, with plenty of fan support from the part of me that said I needed this today.

And it was there, about three sentences past the point where I lurched forward in my chair and said, "So you know what happened?" that I realized it was all out there now. My carefully constructed narratives be damned; the separate silos of facts I kept about the event, depending on who I was talking to—Kyle, his parents, my mom, my good friends, and my not-so-good friends—were all in a heap in the middle of the table at this dive bar, being picked through by people I would have only considered "work friends" before today.

"Oh my god," a very drunk Hannah leaned forward and slapped the table. "*And* your cat died?"

Megan's eye roll could have been seen in the back row of a 10,000-seat theater. "Gawd, no, I just lied about that."

You could see from her wobbling head that Hannah was trying to put the pieces together, and she looked at me to help her. "Wait, so your cat didn't die?"

"She doesn't have a cat!"

Hannah paused, then looked at me again. "Did you ever have a cat?"

I laughed. Perhaps a pity laugh, maybe a drunk laugh, but why analyze it.

"I like cats," Hannah stated, slumping back into the booth. Then she turned to Megan, unfortunately— and unbelievably, considering the state of all of us— returning to the story I had just spilled. "Did you know about this?"

"No."

Both girls turned to me.

In my haze, I thought maybe telling them was a good thing. And Megan and Hannah took their jobs as the sudden recipients of way too much information seriously, as you only can after so much alcohol. We were now blood sisters for life and they were there for me, no matter what I needed. They would not tell anyone at work about it, cross their hearts.

Then Hannah lurched forward again. "Oh! You know whose mom committed suicide? Olivia's!"

I cringed.

When I got back to the motel, some blessed rideshare driver walked me to my door and made sure I at least collapsed on the inside of my door instead of the outside. I locked the door because the driver told me to, and aimed for the dark mass that was my bed. After a minute spread out on the bobbing bed, I realized it would be prudent to move a garbage can and my body closer to the edge of the bed. Fortunately, and perhaps only because I knew I was prepared for it, I did not need it.

The next morning it occurred to me that maybe it was not fortunate that I had not needed the garbage can. I felt awful in every sense of the word. I was sick and spinning, physically and emotionally, and maybe if I could have expelled some of the evil spirits, I would have felt better. The only thing saving me from the beating I was giving myself was that I slept for most of the day.

At some point, when the sun was high in the sky, Sara called. It was a rude awakening and I was immediately nauseous.

"Lauren?"

"Yes, hi!" I sat up, then immediately flopped back into my pillow again, trying to convince my stomach it had never left the minimal expectations of the bed.

"Honey, we're not going to be done moving everything by three o'clock. Can we meet you at the apartment tomorrow instead of today?"

"Oh no, I'm sorry this is taking up your whole weekend." My head ebbed and flowed with the tide of nausea creeping in. And up. I swallowed hard. "Sure, not a problem. Again, thank you so much for doing this." Truthfully, I had forgotten I was supposed to meet them and I doubted I could have done it, but I took this as an unexpected win and tried not to think about it.

"We're happy to help. Say, it's supposed to turn cold tomorrow. Does Kyle have warm clothes for when you pick him up? We can drop something off."

"No, he doesn't have anything, actually." I thought of how I had seen him that day. I assumed that what little he had been wearing had been discarded.

I gave her the name of the motel and said she could leave it with the front desk, thanked her yet again, then hung up and only moved as far as I had to in order to drop my phone from my ear to the bed. I was mercifully asleep again as soon as I closed my eyes.

Then, it was dark out and my phone was ringing again. It was my mom.

"Hi!" I faked perkiness.

"Hi honey, just checking in. Have you moved in to your new apartment?" I realized I had not talked to her for a couple of days.

I sat up with less grimacing than earlier. I told her about losing one apartment then finding another, and about Sara and Alexander handling the move. I left out what I had been doing during that time.

"I'm sorry you lost the other apartment, but that's great you were able to find something else so quickly. And that's so nice of your friends to do that. Make sure you thank them."

I rolled my eyes. "Of course, Mom! You don't think I'm thanking them?" We exchanged some theories on a mother's guiding role in her children's lives versus a child's ability to catch on to social norms at an early age.

Then she asked how Kyle was doing.

"Great. He's doing laps in the pool right now."

"I mean really. Do you know anything yet? You pick him up tomorrow, right?"

"Yeah, I'm supposed to meet with the doctor when I go, so maybe they'll tell me something then."

"Fingers crossed. Give Kyle my love and call me afterward if you want."

"Okay, Mom, thanks."

"I love you honey."

"You too, Mom."

I lay on the bed with the dead phone still held to my ear for a minute. I was trying to picture how tomorrow would go, but it was beyond me.

I woke up early the next morning. I should have expected it after sleeping the day away yesterday, but it now left me with an inordinate amount of time to kill before picking up Kyle.

I huddled in the warm spot in my bed until the last wisp of sleepiness melted away and was rudely replaced by antsiness. I flossed. I brushed my teeth for the full amount of time I should, and then some. I did my hair and makeup like I would if we were going to a nice dinner. That left me nearly out of ideas on how to kill the remaining time.

I waited for the motel office to open so I could get the bag Sara and Alexander left for Kyle; they had dropped it off sometime during the previous evening when I was still wrestling with righting myself. I was embarrassed they had seen the motel where I had been staying.

I peeked through a crack in the curtains, waiting for the *OPEN* sign to blink on. When it did, I opened the door and was left breathless by a shockwave of the cold weather Sara said was coming. I wrapped my arms around myself, darting to the office and wasting no time closing the door behind me.

"Can I help you?" The bulky woman behind the laminate desk had seen me a couple of times but apparently did not immediately recognize me in today's hair and makeup.

"I'm Lauren Delgado in #7. Some friends were supposed to drop off a bag for me yesterday?"

"I'll look." She rocked heavily forward in the chair and pushed herself up, then walked back around a corner. Almost immediately, she came back with Kyle's gym bag with my name on a sticky note stuck to it. "Here you go."

"Thank you." I reached out for the bag and added, "I'll be checking out today, too. I'm leaving in about half an hour."

"Just bring the key here and drop it off when you leave."

"Thank you."

I ran back to my warm room with the bag. Poking through it, I was pleased to see Sara had included shoes for Kyle, since he had gone in without them. I gave a wry smile seeing the sharp outfit Sara had put together for him, knowing he would have never given it that much thought and that it would probably surprise him that it was assembled from his closet.

I stuffed everything back in the bag and set it on the table. Then I set my own bag—which I had bought for my slowly accruing pile of necessities—next to it and started to pack. After checking I had everything for the third time, I backed out of the door, turning off the lights and taking a last look at the little room that had been my main respite. It was not quite bittersweet, but it was neutral ground, and that was enough.

I loaded the bags into my not-quite-nice, not-quite-new car. In my normal life I would forget about it for weeks at a time, opting instead for public transit; in the past few weeks, I had put as many miles on it as I usually would in a year.

I shrunk down into the warmth of my coat as I ran back to the office one last time with the room key. A minute later, I was pulling my still-cold car out of the motel parking lot. I had never thought I would stay here, and I fully expected never to return.

A few minutes later, I drove slowly by a new entrance on the other side of the hospital—my third entrance in as many weeks—and I wondered how many more there were. I squinted at the sign to make sure I was in the right spot, then drove around to the first row to park. I pulled into the parking spot, backed up, and pulled in again straighter. I turned the car off and stared at the entrance. Soon, the cold drove me inside.

I went through the double doors but immediately dead-ended in a reception area that was more of a reception hallway. I walked up to a pleasant-faced woman behind the window. Her voice clicked through the two-way speaker in the middle of the glass. "Good morning. How can I help you?"

"Hi, I'm here to pick up Kyle Hansen?" Why did I say it like a question?

"Your name?"

"Lauren Delgado?" Is it? Is it Lauren Delgado? Because I do not sound sure of that.

"One moment..." She typed on an outdated terminal in front of her. "Okay, you'll be meeting with Dr. Ehrlich first."

"Okay."

"If you want to take a seat, I'll have someone come up and escort you to his office."

"Thank you."

I looked around and saw a few unmatched hard plastic chairs that looked like they had been stolen from the local high school in different eras. I sat in the newest looking one, setting Kyle's bag on the floor next to me.

I shivered. The heat did not appear to be making it past the reception barrier.

About five minutes later, an older man in green scrubs with the fullest head of jet-black hair I had ever seen opened a door in the wall opposite me.

"Ms. Delgado?" His authentic pronunciation of my name made me hold my breath lest I be forced to admit—yet again—that I was a *pocha*, a word I had learned the hard way from the few people around who looked like me when I was growing up. I did not speak the language or know the culture. Another casualty of my father's accident.

I had tried. In high school I signed up for Spanish class with the same woman who had been translating our letters to my *abuela* for years. She acted as if I should know, innately, the words tumbling from her mouth. Trembling, stumbling, trying to get the answer right in front of the class, I felt like a piñata filled with white bread: confusing to see. And confusing to be.

"Again! *Otra vez!*" she commanded, as if she could bully the language into me.

A month into the semester, I asked my mother if I could quit the class. I was shocked when her eyes filled with tears that were heavy with personal failure. "I'm sorry, I should have started us in Spanish classes years ago."

I did not know what to say. Should she have?

She hugged me, and within a week she came back with a supplemental plan full of online classes, videos, radio, and newspapers for us. We posted sticky notes around the house: *puerta*, *refrigerador*, *libro*. We never did master it, but we finished the semester of effort I had committed to. Lesson learned. And she never again used that teacher to translate our *abuela*'s letters.

The man in scrubs was holding the door for me.

"Yes." I quickly gathered my purse and the bag and stood up to follow him, holding my breath. But he just led me, without a word, through a warren of hallways.

I could not take my eyes off his hair. There was so much it seemed there was not enough scalp to contain it properly, and it was sticking out in every direction, with only its length giving the illusion of any style. Was it a toupee? I strained to make out a seam, but could not see one.

Only when we walked past a woman with a clipboard in the hallway watching me stare at the back of his head did I realize how bad I must have looked, and I slowed my pace to walk at a reasonable distance behind him. I did not look back at the woman to see if this had satisfactorily soothed her.

We were headed toward two ominous-looking windowless doors when instead we stopped short and turned into an office located just before them. The man gestured for me to enter as he remained in the hallway to shut the door behind me. The room was warm and clean, if not new. It felt soft and comfortable, with gentle lamp light and fuzzy area rugs and row after row of leather-bound books on honey-colored wood bookshelves. A window opened into a small courtyard where a picnic table waited for warmer days.

A thin man, younger than I expected but not young, stood up from behind a desk in the office and came toward me with his hand outstretched. "Lauren? I'm Dr. Ehrlich."

I shook it.

"So Kyle is going home today."

I nodded and smiled.

"Have a seat, let's talk." He gestured toward a chair and took his own seat behind the desk.

I sat stiffly, clutching the bag, unsure I was ready for this. And twenty minutes later, I still was not sure.

If the cold had chilled me, I was chilled even further by Dr. Ehrlich's warnings about Kyle's increased risk for the next few weeks—do not leave him alone, watch him, make sure he takes his meds, get him to his appointments. It was a mountain of responsibility, outlined neatly on a small packet of papers in front of me, with the ultimate downside for failure.

Finally, Dr. Ehrlich asked if I had any questions. I automatically responded "no," despite the truth. He escorted me out of his office and led me to a chair in a nearby waiting area. He said he would go get Kyle. I squirmed.

"Are those for Kyle? Would you like me to give them to him?" He gestured to the bag of clothes I had in a stranglehold in my lap.

"Oh, yes." I handed him the bag and folded my already-jittery hands across my legs.

Dr. Ehrlich put his hand on my shoulder and I looked up at him. He smiled and nodded. I did the same back to him. It seemed easier to use his emotions in this moment than sort through my own.

I could see him walk back in the direction of his office, then swipe his badge and push through the windowless doors. I wanted, and did not want, this to happen. I focused on my hands as if it was the first time I had ever noticed them. Then I looked again at the doors the doctor had gone through. They gave no indication of what was going on behind them. I drew in a large breath and shifted in the chair.

My mind wandered to our new apartment, wondering if everything would still be packed when we got there. I was happy the bathroom was big. Then I felt guilty for thinking about that at a time like this.

I shifted again in the chair and tried to focus on all the things the doctor had said. I should have thanked him. Why didn't I thank him? I decided to thank him when he came back out. I knew Mom would have told me to thank him.

Then I was exasperated with myself: Kyle is about to leave the hospital and you are thinking about big bathrooms and what Mom would say about your manners.

I sat up straight and looked directly at the door. Be supportive, be loving. Be helpful, but do not treat him like he is helpless. Do not be demanding. Should it be this hard? I mean, this is Kyle we are talking about. I know how to be around Kyle.

I exhaled loudly. Why is it taking so long?

Then: we will probably want to talk about what happened at some point, right? Or do we? Maybe that is something he should talk about with his doctor. If he wants to talk about it with me, I should, but I do not think I bring it up, do I?

I wondered how work was going without me.

Oh my god, just stop it! Do not think about that right now! Think about Kyle!

And then he was there, being pushed out the double doors in a wheelchair by an orderly, Dr. Ehrlich walking alongside him. I stood up, agog, and the purse in my lap dropped to the floor. I snatched it back up and set about wiping the floor off it. Then I stopped and looked at him again, in his great Sara-crafted outfit, and saw him looking at me and smiling his quirky smile. I burst from the inside, releasing an absurd torrent of tears and smiles and laughter.

It was Kyle. And he was coming home with me.

I ran over and wrapped myself around him and he stood up and surrounded me in his impregnable arms, through which I knew nothing bad could get to me.

Dr. Ehrlich looked pleased. "Have a seat, Kyle. Insurance, you know. Let us wheel you outside and you two can be on your way."

Kyle sat back down in the wheelchair, and I pulled away and walked next to him, never taking my eyes off him. He squeezed my hand and smiled. We proceeded out the front door and into the blow of cold air. Outside, Kyle stood again, holding the now-empty gym bag, and the orderly darted away with the wheelchair, back into the warmth of the hospital. The doctor said a few quiet words to Kyle, so quiet that I could not make them out, before clapping him on the back and shaking his hand.

"Thank you, Dr. Ehrlich." Kyle smiled and gave the doctor's hand a strong shake, then released him, too, to the relief of the hospital.

Kyle turned to me and we looked at each other for a pregnant moment, intimate, unsure. To break the strange spell, I reached up and fixed his scarf—I could not believe he had actually put it on—then asked him what he wanted to do before his first appointment later that morning. He smiled and said, "Go for good coffee."

I love this guy.

We walked to a non-chain coffee shop near the hospital that I had been frequenting. It was also near where he had to go for his first follow-up appointment in about an hour. When we walked in, it was full of the usual mix I had seen of medical students studying, professionals enjoying the leisure that follows years of studying, medical staff, and random members of the public who had wandered in.

It felt good to have the barista with the fuzzy hair recognize me and my order, and as Kyle ordered, I focused on finding a table. There were not many good options. It was mid-morning: prime time. I claimed an awkwardly located but open table in the middle of the shop while Kyle waited for the coffees to be offered up to the countertop altar.

We settled in, and Kyle shed his jacket and scarf for the warm, moist air inside the shop. But once he was out from under his scarf, my eyes focused on nothing but the ragged state of his neck.

I looked around. I was not the only one who saw it. Wide eyes and whispers seemed to be traveling around the room like a tsunami.

I wanted to leave and said so.

He was confused. "You want to leave? Why?"

"I just do. Please?" I could not tell him why without exposing myself as the shallow girl more concerned with our image than with how my boyfriend, fresh from the hospital, felt. Even if I did tell him, Kyle never cared how we looked to others. I envied him for that, and occasionally, I let it crawl into my head and root around, upending my confidence that I was someone Kyle could stay with, and that when he really got to know me with all my warts and shortcomings, that would be it.

"Okay." He started fumbling with his jacket, apparently stressed by the sudden pressure to change course.

Abort, abort. This was only attracting more unwanted attention. "No, never mind, this is good."

Kyle stopped fumbling and looked at me with raised eyebrows. "We're staying now?"

"Yeah. I just thought it was too loud in here to talk. And I am excited to see you again. And talk. But this is good."

It made no sense, but he seemed to accept that as an explanation. I was relieved, but then wondered if I normally acted so flighty that this flip-flopping seemed a reasonable thing for me to do.

I pulled Kyle closer by his shirt, under the guise of talking intimately. His large frame pushed the collar of his shirt up to hide what lay under it. We drank our coffees, not too fast but without lingering, and left.

I would have to limit public appearances for a while.

After the coffee shop, I was drained. The morning had all been so much to deal with, and it was only half over. I looked at the time. We were a bit early for his counseling appointment, but that is what a conscientious girlfriend would make sure of, right? I was going to rock my part of this recovery.

Kyle and I walked in silence to the counselor's office building, which was at the edge of the hospital campus near where I had picked him up. I delivered him to the sparse, worn waiting area and sat with him, assured by the receptionist that the counselor would come out at the proper time and take him in. I tried to shake off the feeling I was acting like Kyle's mom instead of his girlfriend.

Kyle sat smiling next to me, with still not much to say. His normal high energy and gregarious personality were M.I.A. It is just the meds they have him on, I decided.

Bored by his passivity, I rifled through the tattered magazines from long-expired subscriptions on the table next to me and studied the cover of one, trying to decide if it was the one for me, but never really delving into it.

About ten minutes later, a portly middle-aged man in a sweater vest came out at exactly the time of the scheduled appointment and called Kyle away.

Step one, complete.

As I waited, crossing and uncrossing my legs, I thought about the afternoon ahead of us. We would go back and find my car in the hospital parking lot, then meet Sara and Alexander at our new building to get the keys to the apartment.

And I had to call Jim. What should I tell him? Weeks? Months? The statistics Dr. Ehrlich shared with me about this period in Kyle's recovery were shocking. Scary.

A big part of me wished I could skip ahead a few months. I was nothing but appreciative of our friends, but I felt like there was an unexploded mine out there somewhere that should have gone off already. Plus, I was not excited to have our friends see Kyle in his current condition. I knew that would be the favorite topic of conversation in our circles for a while to come, and I just wanted to speed through it. At least now I had Kyle to go through it with me.

After the appointment, as we were walking back to find my car, I asked Kyle how the meeting went.

"Fine," he said.

I waited for more, but he did not oblige me.

"Did you like him?"

"He's fine."

I sighed, frustrated. Kyle looked at me. "I'm sorry. I'm thinking about things from the meeting."

"Okay." We walked in silence after that, footsteps crackling on the snow that had become ice overnight, and I looked at Kyle out of the side of my eye, trying to intuit what was going on in there.

We found the car and piled in, filling it with our steamy breath and bulky jackets. I turned the heater on full blast, knowing all it would do is create a cyclone of cold air, but falsely sure it would at least help clear the windows. I waited for it to become effective.

"We're going to head to our new apartment," I said.

Kyle looked straight ahead and nodded and that was that: no questions, no real reaction from him. Just passive acceptance. Medications, I assured myself again.

After a few shivery moments in the car, and a little too soon for true visibility out of the windows, I wound my way out of the parking lot. As I sat at the intersection that would take us away from the medical campus, I looked at the hospital in the rearview mirror and shivered.

It was about fifteen minutes and worlds away when we turned into our new neighborhood. I purposely drove down the cute main street so he could "ooh" and "ahh" at the charm that would now surround us, and while he did look, he said nothing.

Farther down, I pulled into the tiny, crumbling parking lot across from our building and switched off the car. The pavement looked like it could have been deposited before the Last Ice Age, but it had mature, reaching trees waiting to provide shade in the summer, and noble old buildings all around. It was a pleasant contrast from the neighborhood of shiny metal high-rise buildings we had lived in before. I paused before getting out to let him take it all in.

He looked at me. "Ready?"

"Yeah," I said, disappointed.

We jaywalked from the parking lot to our new place. Sara and Alexander were out front, arms crossed against the cold, waiting with the keys. It occurred to me that Alexander should have been at work, and that my debt to them got a little bigger. Was he there just to hand over the keys? Or was he there to protect Sara from the awkwardness of this situation?

"Is that Sara? And Alexander?" Kyle asked.

"Yeah," I said as we walked up. We exchanged all the normal greetings and I noticed they were careful to keep their eye contact at head level. Kyle was quiet. I made up for it with franticness. It was the first time I had seen them since they had been to our old apartment.

I thanked them extravagantly for all they had done, without reference to the impetus for it, as if we had won our new apartment on a game show.

"You're all set!" Alexander dropped the key into my gloved hand, then they waved goodbye to let us get settled in and ease their own discomfort.

We walked up rather than take the squirrelly elevator, which may have fit two people a hundred years ago, but was a squeeze with modern humans and certainly with someone as tall as Kyle.

Walking up the stairs, I was not sure what to expect when we opened the door. Stacks of boxes waiting for us? Please, not all our friends waiting to yell "Welcome home!" to Kyle. I held my breath and balked for a moment before continuing.

Finally, opening the door, I exhaled.

It was our previous life laid out in a happy new way in this happy new apartment to give us the best possible homecoming, and one that would in no way remind us of the place from which we had departed. I was amazed how much work they had put into it, even down to re-hiding the record I bought Kyle for his birthday in the back of my closet.

"What do you think?" I asked.

"This is nice. Thank you." He hugged me sexlessly, then turned away.

Okay...?

We walked around, changing a few things to reflect our inefficient preferences, and I silently noted the few items appropriately missing. I was sorry and relieved our friends had to deal with them. I also wondered what became of them, picturing them on the curb with a *FREE* sign. But maybe they deserved a fresh start, too. We were all trying to escape the event.

Kyle walked through the apartment but did not seem to have any questions about how this had all been accomplished or who knew what. Perhaps it was easier not to talk about it.

After I ordered some furniture shuffled around, I stood back and looked at the new arrangement with satisfaction. Kyle sat on the couch, hands folded politely in his lap, looking around like it was a showroom, not his new home. I picked up one of his arms and curled up under it as I plopped down next to him. I looked up at him with a clear, unspoken demand for a kiss, which he willingly provided.

I was glad he was home.

That night, I lay in bed looking out the window at the naked tree branches exposed by the glare of the streetlights, listening to the sounds of our new neighborhood. I should have been asleep hours ago, but here I lay, just me and my racing mind.

Kyle was breathing loudly—almost snoring—and I rolled over to look at him. I knew every line of his body, though they were subtly changed by weeks of inactivity during his recovery. I inched closer, enjoying the smell of him that had been absent from my life for the past few weeks. It was a smell that marked so many of my best memories with him—his arms wrapped all the way around me when I was crying and a little scared after I had a fender bender in my car; him tan and sweating during whatever game he and his friends were playing that day; and other times when it was just us, skin on skin, finding delight in each other.

A train horn sounded its way through the industrial part of town and I fondly noted it was the same one that woke me up at this time of night at our old apartment, though farther away. Sometimes it would wake Kyle up, too, and it would be the start of something. I waited to see if tonight would be one of those nights—those electric, sweaty nights—but he did not stir. Still, I relaxed into it all, and together the sounds, smells, and memories formed a comforting mélange that nudged me toward sleep.

We had to deal with an initial surge of medications and appointments—doctors, physical therapy, speech therapy, counselors. I had a checklist.

Plus, almost immediately, Kyle's parents and his two younger brothers made a special trip out to see him and not talk about the event. His family wore strained, put-on smiles under their watery eyes, and tried to infuse lightness into the conversations with meaningless chitchat that alternately bored them to figurative tears and moved them to real tears with its awkwardness.

For me, they only ever had jokes about things in the "big city" and comments about the fact I wore heels when I went out. I pretended to be put out at dealing with them on top of the busy schedule, but I was secretly happy to not be alone with all of it, no matter what they thought of my "fancy" shoes.

Kyle's voice had not totally returned, and the strain of the constant activity and conversation during his family's visit was exacerbating it, requiring additional treatment and doctoral admonishments to rest it.

Kyle's main doctor, Dr. Ehrlich, encouraged me to keep him apprised of how Kyle was doing between appointments, and I treated the request like a commandment, to the point where his staff eventually assured me they were glad he was doing well, and that I could now just give them updates on the major things.

I took great delight in ticking things off the checklist, knowing each one represented us inching closer to normal.

We spent most of the time with his family together in the new apartment, which was perfect for two people but quite cozy with six. Thankfully, his family had rooms in a nearby chain hotel, so we only had to work around each other during the daytime hours.

Typically, when we were around his family, we seemed to break into two groups, the men and the women—but since his mom was sovereign of the men as well, she'd drift off to that group. So that left me alone in my own group, with Kyle constantly attempting defection to join me. This time, however, his family knocked me off-balance in a flash flood of unsolicited gratitude, and after three days of tearful private hugs, I found myself missing the peace of his mother's prior thinly veiled disapproval of me.

On the fourth day of their visit, a Saturday, Kyle, his dad, and brothers were sprawled around the living room watching reruns of old games, cheering as if the results depended on it, with Kyle clapping fiercely to save his voice. They looked like a time-lapse movie, showing one man at various phases of his life, instead of four different men. His dad, Chuck, was what Kyle would be in thirty years. Looking at his brothers was looking at Kyle seven and nine years ago. It was as if their mother was not genetically involved at all.

I was lost in the scene when his mother inserted herself to ask for my help in the kitchen: an obvious cover, for many reasons. I tried to catch Kyle's attention on the way out of the room for a little joint eye-rolling, but he apparently had not noticed the opportunity.

In the kitchen, his mother breathed in deeply and smoothed her hair back in a way that reminded me of Kyle's favorite David Bowie album cover. I made a mental note to tell him about it later.

Hair restored and composure regained, she reached out for my hand. Her soft yet crinkly skin unnerved me, and I wanted to pull my hand away but did not.

"I think Kyle should move back home to convalesce."

To heal in the warmth of your smothering bosom, I thought, but said nothing.

She continued, "He is going to have a tough enough time taking care of himself, let alone you. It would be good for him to get away from the situation."

The situation that caused this, she may as well have said. At least the disapproval was back.

I feigned surprise that this trip to the kitchen had any designs other than the stated kitchen assistance, and it gave me a moment to apply the requisite amount of respect to my ready answer. "Having you here right now really has been helpful, and I know he is so glad to see you all, but his doctors and therapists are all here, and they say he is making good progress."

"But you'll be going back to work soon, and he'll be left here by himself. At home I can be there with him."

Oh yeah, he'd love that. Deep breath. "The doctors say he can go back to work soon, too. He's doing really well here."

"Oh yes, *very* well."

Oh. Right. Not really well, I guess.

That night in bed I sidled up to his back and pressed my nose against him. "Your mom wants you to come home."

"Oh? When did she tell you this?"

"Today, when she asked me to help her in the kitchen." I smiled into his back, ready to reclaim the humor we had missed earlier that day, but once again it sailed easily by.

And soon he was snoring.

It looked like my Kyle's-mom-as-Bowie imitation would have to wait.

Kyle's family filled him with all the emergency love and confidence they could without alluding to the reason for it, then left. They were flying out on Valentine's Day, and while I knew I would have to forgo any expectations of romanticism from Kyle this year, it was a happy day nonetheless.

I thought it strange how buoyed he was by their visit when usually these family visits just spurred on a new slew of jokes about why he moved so far away from them. It is different when you are sick, I thought, and checked it off my internal list, glad it and the half hour of tearful hugging and pressure to make promises to each other in the airport were done.

That also meant we would finally have some time to ourselves.

I loved the fact that our new apartment was in a great, old part of the city. I was eager to explore the neighborhood, and I dragged Kyle around mercilessly, as if there would be a test on it later. We found coffee shops with good vibes and local art, and lively bars where we could meet our friends. We found chic, dim restaurants with inviting happy hours, and the most convenient grocery store.

We were exhilarated. Well, I was exhilarated, and he seemed content enough to smile at my excitement. He was still recovering and got tired quicker than he used to. We spent more time at home in front of the television than out and about these days. I looked forward to getting back to full steam, being full of ourselves and full of each other. Like it had been.

Kyle's throat had been healing, though slowly. Mostly I knew that from his strengthening support for the teams on television, not from any stimulating conversations we were having.

A couple of weeks later, on a day when I was particularly bored and fidgety, Kyle suggested I invite my mom to visit, since she was back from Italy. "You'd probably have more fun exploring with her than me." It was a cover. Kyle loved my mom as much as I did.

I was happy to extend the invitation and she was delighted to accept.

"I would love to see you both. Are you sure I wouldn't be intruding?"

"No, his family already took care of that."

"Oh honey, you can be so mean."

"I'm just kidding. Kyle was happy they came."

"Oh? That's a change." I was surprised even Mom realized that. "But then, it's always comforting to have family around during trying times."

"I guess. I just felt like they made it more trying."

She clicked her disapproval. "I hope you didn't act like that to them. You were raised better than that."

"Don't worry, I had them sign a waiver that relieves you of responsibility for any and all social failings I may exhibit."

She laughed. "That's a relief. Act any way you like, then."

•

Two days later, I sat like a cat in the window, watching for her. Then she was there, getting out of the car, her tiny form bundled head-to-toe against the sunny but cold not-quite-spring day, thanking the driver for getting her bags, and smiling up at our new building. I sprinted down to the front door to let her in before she even started up the steps.

"Mom!" I flung open the door and ran down.

She laughed and dropped her bags to wrap herself around me. It was one of her best qualities— her amazing, heartfelt hugs.

After we peeled apart, I appreciated her "fresh from Italy" bronzy glow. "You look great, Mom! And did you lose a few pounds? Who loses weight on a vacation?" She deflected with her usual modesty and attributed any improvement to poor light. No wonder I never learned to take a compliment.

I picked up her bags and started up the stairs, plunging into weeks' worth of pent-up conversation, even though we talked every few days. She just laughed and puffed a little as we climbed to the fourth floor. "How can you talk and climb these stairs!"

"I guess we could have taken the elevator."

"*Now* you tell me!"

Kyle met us at the landing on our floor and bear-hugged her, smiling.

Mom pulled away and, looking up and holding him at arms' length, pleasure apparent, said, "I am so happy to see you, sweetheart." She then pulled him in for another hug. Kyle grinned and let himself be cuddled by her. And if I were the emotional type, which I am not, I may have choked up a bit at the scene.

He grabbed her bags from me and ushered her into our apartment. She gave his arm a loving squeeze as he held the door open for her.

Mom glowed even brighter than the branch-filtered sun lighting up our windows. "Oh yes, this is lovely. Just lovely. What a perfect little nest for you two."

She walked around, cooing at every charming detail and sun-dappled surface. "Yes, Sara did a beautiful job decorating. I'm just sorry you didn't thank her for it."

Mom and I laughed, and Kyle smiled, accepting that it was a moment just for us.

We stashed Mom's suitcases by the door to be dealt with later. She was staying at the most picturesque of bed-and-breakfasts just a few blocks from our apartment. It was in one of the few grand old Colonials sprinkled throughout the neighborhood that had not been divided up into condos. One look at it and you could see the amazing history of the place. But we would not let her head there yet.

"So, was Italy amazing?" I plunked down on the couch, pulling her down next to me.

Mom giggled. "Sì, è stato fantastico."

I grinned and wrinkled my nose. "Whaaaaaat? Did you learn Italian??"

She laughed. "No, not really. I learned a few phrases because, you know, one should try when you go to their country."

Kyle was still standing behind us, smiling, but I saw him edging back toward the television. I grabbed his hand. "No, don't watch TV."

"That's all right honey, let him watch. He doesn't need to hear about my trip."

I turned to Kyle and did my best imitation of a TV gangster. "Are you calling my mom boring, Kyle?"

He went serious and looked almost worried. "No!"

"Let him go, honey."

I looked at Kyle and furrowed my brow. "I'm just kidding." I searched his face for the subtle wink or eye roll that would tell me we were participating in the same skit. But no, nothing.

My mom grabbed my hand. "But let me tell you about the coast of *Italy*!"

I smiled at her. I wanted to hear about the Italian coast, and I treasured this time with my mom, but it did not escape my attention that Kyle sidled back over in front of the television, and I was irritated by his departure.

The three of us spent the rest of the afternoon chatting in the apartment. Well, Mom and I chatted while Kyle sat on the couch with one ear on our conversation but both eyes on the game he was watching without sound. Every once in a while, Kyle would hoarsely shout something to the game, startling Mom and me.

He would look over at us looking at him and become small. "Sorry."

My mom just laughed and squinted at the television. "Is this some sort of championship game?"

"No, it's—"

"A twenty-year-old game!" I interrupted. "Can't you watch that another time? Mom's only here for a couple of days!"

Kyle and Mom both looked at me, and Mom said, "You know this game? I didn't know you watched basketball."

"No, I don't. I mean, but look at the length of the shorts and the style of the shoes!"

Kyle and Mom both looked at the television, then looked at me again.

"Come on, that's clearly...well, when is it from?"

He thought for a second. "Twenty-two years ago."

"Give the fashions a year to go mainstream and that's almost twenty years."

Mom burst into laughter. "Honey, you spend too much time shopping."

Kyle smiled.

It was impossible to hold on to my indignation with my mom around. I sighed. "I'm hungry, what's our plan for dinner?"

Kyle switched off the television, finally. "Do you want to order in?"

I pouted, but my mom—always the peacemaker—chimed in, "Actually, I wouldn't mind that. I had an early train and I still have to go get settled in my room later." Then she turned back to me and put her hand on my leg. "But I'd love to try whatever you want. My treat."

Sigh. Just impossible.

We ended up having a fun night of games and wine and great food at the apartment. Mom taught us a card game she learned during her trip to Italy and left us the beautifully illustrated deck she had purchased there.

The next day, Mom and I went to get to know the neighborhood. I took her to a couple of spots I had already found on my explorations with Kyle, as well as a couple of spots Kyle could not be persuaded to try.

One of the latter was a little café with delicate wire seats and tiny tables that would hold a sandwich but preferred a cappuccino. I could see Kyle's point: he would have looked a little ghoulish trying to fold himself into that arrangement. But for us it was the perfect mid-day break.

"Ahh!" Mom said as she settled into a seat, hanging her coat on the back of it and setting her shopping bags down beside her. "I believe I'll have to buy another travel bag to get all my new treasures home. And you didn't do too badly yourself."

I looked in my single bag with its few inhabitants. "Yeah, I really like everything I got. And thanks again for buying us that rug for the entryway. You didn't have to do that, especially considering how much help you already gave us getting this apartment."

"But it was so perfect. And I wanted to buy you something you really wanted for a housewarming present."

I smiled. "Thanks, Mom. I'll send you pictures of how it looks after we pick it up."

"Are you sure Kyle didn't want to join us? I feel bad leaving him behind."

"No, he is only too happy to let you take his place on these excursions. He'd rather stay home and watch sports."

Mom did not say anything, but nodded and waited for me to go on, ready to listen if I was ready to talk. But I was not looking for an opportunity to bad-mouth

Kyle, just to squeeze in a few superficial grumblings, so I let the opportunity pass.

"We'll all go out to dinner tonight," I said, moving on.

Mom smiled again, but not as freely. "Only on the condition that you let me pay."

"Deal." All this time off work was not exactly going unnoticed in my bank account.

"So, things are good? Kyle is doing well?" It was surprisingly forward for my mother.

I let myself be distracted by the menu the server placed in front of me. "He's coming along. The doctors say it can be a slow road. That omelet looks good."

"Have you guys talked about it?" Her question surprised me, though I do not know why it would have.

I dropped my eyes from the menu, but did not look at my mom. "No, not yet."

Mom put her hand on my arm and gave it a pat, then gave me a smile. "I just wish you would tell Sara thank you."

We both laughed. In that moment, I loved my mom even more for letting me off a hook I was not ready to be on.

Mom let me pick where to go for dinner that night, of course. I left her at the bed-and-breakfast to "freshen up," and I headed home to get changed and collect Kyle.

I opened the door to the apartment with the flourish born of a great day. "Hellooo!" I sang, setting my bag and coat on the bench near the front door.

Kyle turned around to see me from his place on the couch. "Where's your mom?"

"I left her at the bed-and-breakfast. She's going to change and, I think, sneak in a little nap." I sat down on the bench and started peeling off my shoes. "But we need to change. Mom's taking us to dinner."

"Oh."

"Oh?"

"Okay."

"I mean, you knew we'd be doing dinner together, right?"

"I don't know. I thought maybe you and your mom... and there's a game on...."

"Nooo!" I threw down my shoe. "All you've been doing is watching whatever game is on. You can skip one game and go to dinner with us while my mom is visiting."

"Okay, okay. I'll record it." He turned back around toward the television.

I waited for some movement from him toward the bedroom. "Are you wearing that to dinner? Because I think it will limit the places we can go."

Big sigh from Kyle. Then a grunt as he stood up and went to the bedroom to change. I followed him in.

Kyle stared at his closet as if it was the first time he had seen one.

"Here. Wear this." I plucked a shirt from its hanger and grabbed a pair of pants from his stack of "not sweats" and threw them both down on the bed.

He started changing, obediently, if not enthusiastically, and I turned to my own clothing dilemma. I paged through the hangers on my side of the inadequately sized closet. "Did people really have so few clothes a hundred years ago?"

"Huh?" My question had stopped his progress.

"Nothing, nothing."

Eventually, we both emerged, ready for any dress code that could be found in our neighborhood. I called to let Mom know we were leaving the apartment, to give her enough time to be ready after the nap I was sure she was taking.

"Did I wake you?" I asked.

"No, no!" Yes. Mom would never admit to taking a nap. "Your timing is perfect, I'm almost ready. I'll meet you out front. I'm looking forward to dinner with you two."

My mom was amazing to me. How could she squeeze in so many ways to make me feel wonderful? Did she do that for everyone?

We strolled slowly over to where Mom was staying, and she popped out the front door, smiling and waving, just as we got there. She must have been watching for us from her room.

"Don't you look beautiful!" she said to me as she approached. "And Kyle...so handsome." We both beamed.

We headed to a nearby restaurant. Kyle and I had browsed the menu before and liked it, but it was a bit out of our price range for a regular spot, so we had been saving it for when our parents were buying.

It was another great night of conversation. At least for Mom and I. Even without the distraction of the television, Kyle did not contribute a lot. I was irked he did not seem to be trying to make Mom's trip more fun, but she did not seem to notice, so I tried to let it go.

I was sure my mom would want to head back to her room after dinner, but to my pleasant surprise she accepted my offer to come up to our apartment for an after-dinner drink.

"That would be lovely, if it's not too much of an imposition." That was clearly the cue for Kyle and I to jointly protest such an idea and insist she join us, but I found myself protesting alone while Kyle walked quietly along.

I nudged Kyle and flashed him an unhappy, meaningful look.

"What?" he said.

I rolled my eyes and glared at him for ruining it.

"Or maybe another time?" Mom was backtracking now.

"No, Mom, come up."

"Are you sure?"

"Absolutely," I said. Kyle was the one I did not want up there right now, not my mom.

Mom came up, accepted only the smallest pour of wine, and then made excuses to get back to her room. And as soon as she said the words, Kyle flipped on the television. I was so annoyed with him. There was plenty of usable evening left and my mom was leaving in the morning, so I was not happy about her early exit. I protested, but I knew she was too gracious to stay longer. I insisted on walking her back, without Kyle.

Outside on the tree-lined street, the temperature had already dropped, reminding me that even though the day had been gently warm, it was still early spring. Despite her downy jacket and scarf, Mom shivered. I linked arms with her.

"What time are you heading to the station tomorrow?"

"I should leave around nine."

"Do you want to get a coffee first?"

"I think I'll just grab something at the bed-and-breakfast in the morning, if that's okay. I don't know how I'm going to get everything packed. I shouldn't have bought so many things."

I pursed my lips, sure this was Kyle's fault.

"We'll at least come see you off at nine."

We were already in front of the bed-and-breakfast when Mom turned to face me. "Okay, if you want. But don't be too hard on him, okay? He's been through a lot."

I grumbled. Mom pulled me in and hugged me hard. "Promise me."

"Okay." I was not committed to the idea, but I knew my mom would not want to feel like she was the reason for any discord. I watched her walk up the beautiful steps toward the front door, thinking how perfect she looked among the graceful columns and elegant landscaping.

At the top, she turned and waved and I could hear her voice floating over to me. "I love you, honey."

I waved back, and she turned to go in.

I started walking back toward our apartment, rehearsing what I would say to Kyle. But when I swung the door open, he was not in front of the television like I had expected him to be. Instead, he emerged from the bedroom, already in his boxers, brushing his teeth for bed.

While he ducked back into the bathroom to rinse, I sat on our bench in the entryway for a minute, shedding my shoes. I tried to take to heart what my mom had said and revised the speech I had rehearsed.

Before I could launch into it, though, Kyle came back out and stood in front of me. "I'm sorry, I'm really tired tonight."

"You could have made my mom feel more welcome on her last night here! Why didn't you ask her to come up for a nightcap?"

"You asked her."

"I mean, why didn't you say you wanted her to come up, too?"

"I don't know. I'm tired."

"You couldn't have just done it to be polite? She's leaving in the morning!"

Kyle stood there looking at me, but said nothing. I could see the color rise where the skin on his neck was still healing. I looked down and sighed.

I walked into the bedroom and changed into my flannel jammie pants and a t-shirt. Kyle followed me in. I walked into the bathroom to brush my teeth and by the time I was done he was already in bed, lying on his side facing away from me. I flipped back the covers and climbed in on the other side, also lying on my side away from him.

The bed bounced slightly and I realized he had rolled over toward me. "I'm sorry, Lauren. I love your mom, and I'm sorry I wasn't polite."

It sounded odd, but heartfelt.

I rolled halfway over, lying on my back, to look at him. His eyes looked sad.

"It's okay." Then, even though I had determined I did not want him to come in the morning, I added, "Do you want to come with me to see her off in the morning?"

"Yes." He looked relieved.

I smiled up at him, thinking this tender moment may flower into something else, but he settled back down on his side of the bed, and soon I heard his gentle snoring.

The next morning, just before nine, Kyle and I walked up to see Mom standing on the sidewalk with two very full bags.

She waved and smiled when she saw us, and we quickened our steps, as if she might leave before we got to her. "I'm so glad I got to come visit you two."

Kyle spoke first. "We love having you. I'm sorry I wasn't polite last night, and I wish you could stay longer."

My mom did not seem to notice the awkwardness of his apology. She smiled at him and waved off the invitation. "Guests are only fun to have when they leave a little too soon." She laughed at her own joke, and then reached up for a hug from Kyle.

I raised an eyebrow. "That is an idea that has never crossed the mind of Kyle's parents."

Kyle stared at me mid-hug, and Mom chided me for saying such a thing.

I was as surprised at Kyle's reaction as I had been sure of hers. "Wow, okay, sorry."

A car pulled up next to us, clearly here for my mother. Kyle did not say anything to me but turned to talk to the driver, then started loading her bags into the trunk.

Mom turned to me and grabbed my hands in hers. "Honey, you know you can call me any time."

"I know, Mom."

She continued to hold my gaze, but I cut it short by coming in for my hug. "I love you, Mom."

"I love you, too. SO much." She gave me a squeeze.

Kyle came over, smiling, reporting that Mom was packed and ready to go. He opened the car door for her, and she gave me a small wave and stepped in, thanking Kyle for minding the door.

Kyle and I waved after her car as she drove away, until we could no longer make out the kisses she was blowing us through the window.

I was still looking after the car when I said, "Thank you for saying that to my mom."

We turned and walked back toward our apartment.

In the next days and weeks, we continued to conscientiously work on completing our checklists. We worked hard to ask the right questions and meet our goals. Also, we noticed things—or rather, I noticed things.

Whenever I saw things that would be in the way of getting back to normal, I added them to one of two lists of questions I had for the doctor. Some, *we* would ask about: his voice, his stamina. Others, *I* would ask about: he seems so passive—is that the drugs? I felt a twinge of dishonesty about having separate lists, and I asked my mom about it one day.

"Do you think I should have Kyle there when I'm asking the doctor my questions? I feel like I'm talking about him behind his back."

"I can see why you might feel disloyal, but I don't think anyone else will think that. I certainly don't. Right now, you are trying to help Kyle, and yourself, heal. Don't forget you need some support here, too."

"Yeah..."

"Honey, I know you love Kyle and you are trying to be there for him. This is me loving you and trying to be there for you."

"I know. Thanks, Mom. I'm sorry you hate Kyle."

"Honey! That is not at all—!"

I laughed.

"Oh, I see. Torment the old lady."

"You are NOT old!"

"You are making me old!" She was laughing now, too. Then she added, "I think you'll know when it's something you should have Kyle there for."

"Thanks, Mom. I love you."

"I love you, too, honey."

I went back to work the next day. Even if I was not that excited about working, I was looking forward to a break from what was turning into a pretty tedious comeback process. Besides, Jim was not going to hold my job for me forever.

I arrived to our reception-less employee-only floor, predictably twenty minutes late, but armed with the new excuse that I had to figure out the bus from my new apartment. I slipped in and skirted the edges of the oceanic room that housed those of us working our way up—or not—from the bottom rung. We were not all working in the same department, but in some org-chart kind of way we all worked together, therefore we were co-located with them. The future overthrowers like Megan, Hannah and I were situated in the middle of the worknasium in a maze of half-walled cubicles, where our managers, who were officed in a beltway surrounding the maze, could keep an eye on us.

I froze when I rounded the last corner to my cubicle and saw my computer and chair were covered in a schizophrenic collage—cards, cutesy memes that had undoubtedly been researched and printed on company equipment, balloons, a small stuffed cat with a heart-shaped necklace that read *wuv you*, chocolate, and strangely enough, a bobblehead.

Of all things. A bobblehead.

How, exactly, had Jim explained my absence? What else did he say besides that I had a "family emergency"? What kind of details had Megan and Hannah added to that description? I looked around, hoping no one had seen me come in.

No such luck.

All around me people were peeking their heads up, looking to see my initial reaction to their outpouring. I realized they had been waiting for this and there would be no robbing them of it.

I reached blindly for one of the cards and opened it, as if looking for the key to get back through the wormhole I had just fallen through: *Get well.* I guess my exact situation is not on Hallmark's list of top twenty life events. Deep breath.

Unwillingly, I reached for the bobblehead. With a churning stomach, I watched its head whip back and forth as I picked it up from my chair, then realized with a shock that my trembling hand was causing the movement, and abruptly dropped it. It rolled limply under the chair, resting with its head at a sickening angle.

I could not do this. I turned blindly to make my escape but was stopped by a friendly blockade of people starting to gather to welcome me back. I started to sweat. My head and stomach were in a tailspin, and I let my weak knees lower me onto the edge of my chair to avoid a worse alternative, remembering the bobblehead only when I heard the crunch. My co-workers ohhh'd sadly at the ruined little figure, and one crouched down to retrieve the pieces.

Inexplicably, she held them out to me until I allowed them to be poured into my cupped hands. It was then I realized for the first time the bobble was of a comedian I liked.

Not so funny now.

"I...I...need to use the restroom." I dropped the broken bobble pieces on my desk and practically ran out to the hall where the bathrooms were. Sweating and weak, I chose the private "family" bathroom (where lactating co-workers built up their babies' food supplies) so I could have the space to myself. I locked the door solidly behind me and leaned against it, trying to hold my breath to minimize the bathroom air I took into my lungs.

I could not stay here.

I unlocked the door and looked through the crack. No one was there, and I had a clear view of the doorway to the back stairs. I made a quick exit from the bathroom, dead set on making a successful escape. A woman who worked near me, but who I had not talked to yet that morning, had been headed to the ladies' room but changed direction toward me when she saw me. I waved at her, but kept going toward the door. I heard her calling my name but kept going, only increasing my speed—out the door, down the stairs, only one more flight, then outside!

I was breathing hard, and I was not sure if it was from my escape or the situation I was escaping from. I wished I had grabbed my phone so I could call my mom, but I knew that going out of your way to take your phone with you when you said you were going to the bathroom could be a weird thing that would dog you for the rest of your work life, so I decided it was good that I had not. I walked down the sidewalk, hugging myself for warmth, and focused on breathing in the only-recently-not-cold-but-not-yet-warm-either spring air. It helped clear my head but it was not warm enough to spend much time outside without a jacket.

As my breathing returned to normal and my stomach stopped its Tilt-A-Whirl ride, I looked around and placed myself on the back side of our office building. There was a small surface parking lot devoid of cars, and butted up against the landscaping was a strange little bus stop-like structure for—I am guessing—smokers. It was empty at the moment, and from the looks of it had transitioned to disuse as newer generations of tobacco products and people had gone in different directions. But there it sat, just in case.

I kept a slow pace up and down the sidewalk until I felt it had scrubbed me clean, and I could try this again.

I pulled at the door I came out of, knowing before I tugged on it that it would be locked. I followed the sidewalk back around to the front of the building, wondering which people higher on the organizational chart were sitting behind the windows, watching my little scene unfold. At least it is no one I work with, I thought, picturing our windowless work area.

I went back through the front doors, rode the elevator to our floor, and stepped off, renewed. Even with that, I was relieved when I realized that my awkward exit had not been noticed, and the alarm bells clanging around my ears had only been broadcasting inside my head.

My boss, Jim, was walking toward me on the other side of a row of cubicles and spotted me heading back to my desk. He flashed me a huge smile and raised a motionless hand in the air as a greeting. "Glad to have you back, Lauren."

I raised an awkward, similarly frozen hand as if my arm had turned into a flipper, and gave him a grimacing smile. I settled back into my cubicle and sat in front of my computer, ready for the next round. My courage faltered slightly when I had not even been able to adjust myself in my seat before someone was there again, but I steeled myself and smiled appreciatively at the next comer.

The next few hours were a repeating series of squirmy encounters with my co-workers, one after another, each with their own well-intentioned attempt to show they cared. Every time I turned around to see them, I could see the queue of people circling around behind them, waiting to catch me alone next.

Worse, the remnants of the bobble were still on my desk. I did not know what to do with them. I knew they needed to go in the garbage, but I felt strange sweeping them into the waste bin in front of my co-workers. At the same time, I could not go on answering questions about what had happened to it, either.

Right before lunch, Megan and Hannah appeared in my doorway with sympathetic smirks on their faces.

"You ready to get out of here?" Megan said. I swept the bobble shards into the garbage, grabbed my coat from its shoulder-high cubicle-top-hook and pushed past them.

"So that's a yes?" Megan laughed after me.

At lunch, ensconced in the safety of a deep faux-leather booth, I gulped down my first martini before Megan and Hannah had even finished running through the usual litany of substitutions in their food orders. As I ordered a second one, the waitress's enthusiasm gave way to wariness.

"It's okay. It's her first day back at work," Hannah said by way of justification. The waitress nodded, then frowned, but had the good sense to just walk away.

Megan frisbeed a greeting-card envelope across the table at me. Great, more cards. It lay there as I glared at her. "Seriously?"

"Open it."

You look like crap. Work on that, it read. I tried to maintain my head of resentment but smiled in spite of myself. Still there was something I could not let go. "Who left the bobblehead?" I trembled again just thinking about it.

"Bobblehead? I don't know. Someone really left you a bobblehead?" Hannah seemed stressed at the idea.

"No big deal," I lied.

"I'm sorry, Lauren." Hannah laid her hand on my arm. "They don't know what the 'family emergency' was. I'm sure they would never have done that if they knew."

At least that information had not gotten out. I tried another tack. "So hopefully no one at work noticed everything went smoothly without me."

"Not totally smoothly," Megan looked thoughtfully at Hannah, "but probably well enough that you should object to the state of 'things' now that you're back."

"Good idea," I said.

Lunch progressed, after a long and likely purposeful delay in getting my next martini. Mostly we talked of work and the people there. I braced myself for the obvious questions that would surely come, but they never did. They gossiped about co-workers, complained about managers, and planned their weekends, but they never asked any more about the thing that had kept me out of work all these weeks, the thing that had led to our blood-alcohol-sisterhood.

It struck me as strange they would not ask about it.

Nearly two hours later, the level of effort required to break free from staring at the bottom of my third martini made me realize I should just email Jim that the day had been too hard on me, and I was taking the afternoon off.

It was not a total lie.

With a parting reminder of a floor meeting we had in the morning, Hannah and Megan headed back to work, leaving me there to puzzle after them.

I sighed and headed in the opposite direction, toward home.

A short time later, I practically fell through the door to the apartment, not even turning around to dislodge the kicked-off shoe that stood in the way of closing the door, instead stretching a toe from where I sat on the entryway bench to flip it into the corner.

I heard the television on in the living room. "You here?" I called.

"Yeah." Kyle was sitting on the couch watching sports.

"My kingdom for a martini!"

"Isn't it a little early?"

"Aren't YOU a little early?" I could hear the slur in my response.

I did not hear anything for a second, but then came a grunt as he got up from the couch without comment and went to the kitchen to make me the requested martini.

I walked into the living room and collapsed dramatically on the poufy chair opposite his favorite sofa indentation, hair down and already half out of my work clothes. "That was easy," I mocked.

No comment from the kitchen.

A second later he was there, a bland smile on his face, handing me my cocktail.

"I see why you white guys were reluctant to give this up."

He sat back down in the place I guessed he had occupied all day, with the best view of the television. I swung my legs up and wiggled my toes enticingly at him. He sighed and began to rub my feet, eyes on the TV.

"Boy, you are a total pushover today. I'd better not let you answer the door in case the Girl Scouts are out selling cookies." I turned to switch out feet. "But in case you do...Samoas. I don't care what the Thin Mint lobby says."

"How was work? You're home early." He patted my feet in the universal signal for *the massage is now over*.

I paused. So far this was a conversation I could have had with my boss, not one I expected from my intelligent, witty boyfriend. "It sucked. My talents are being squandered on the unappreciative." I wanted to tell him about my horrible day with the bobblehead and my thoughtful yet Chupacabrian co-workers, but stopped myself.

"Well, it's your first day back." Except for making my martini, he had not looked away from the television since I came home.

This was not the homecoming I had been looking forward to. I sat up under the guise of taking a drink of my as-yet-untouched martini, to look at what he found so interesting on the television. Guys talking sports, as far as I could tell. "Football?"

"Basketball."

I was pretty sure I should have known that. Maybe I did know that. I sipped at my drink and stole a glance at him and softened. "How was your day?"

He looked at me, but his look was undecipherable. "It was fine." His gaze fell back to the television.

I narrowed my eyes. "Are you okay?"

"Yeah." He looked at me briefly and attached a smile to his response this time, but it felt like he was just looking for the right combination of responses and reactions to satisfy me. I guess this had always been what he had done, what men have done, but shouldn't he be better at it? This guy had unlocked my combination years ago.

"I'm going to change." I heaved myself out of the chair and headed for the bedroom, sloshing a little of my drink on the way. Once there, I sat on the edge of the bed and thought about the day. Why did I stop myself from talking to him about it? It was the right decision, but why?

Better to not think about it, said the martinis.

The next day at work was not as bad except I had a bit of a headache from the previous day's martini-centric activities, and I actually had to get some work done. I also noticed a new prominence in my mid-section from all the *taking it easy* we had been doing lately, so I also committed to going to the gym after work to complete my triumphant return.

By the time I got off work my motivation had waned, but I forced myself to go anyway, knowing I would never get there if it was that easy to worm my way out of it. Once I started, I was happy I did it, but it was a battle getting myself there and my stamina was sorely lacking. I justified a short workout with "not doing too much too fast" and headed out.

The weather was warming up, comparatively speaking, and I decided to walk home from the gym, to get a little fix of the day's last sunshine. On the way, I called my mom.

"Hi, honey!"

"Hi, Mom!"

"To what do I owe this honor?"

"Just walking home from work and the gym."

"You didn't tell me you started back to work! How was it? Nice to get out of the apartment?"

"Well, yesterday was awful." I related the short, edited version of the previous day's events, leaving out the subsequent martini-fest.

"I'm sorry, honey. You know they meant well. It's hard for people to know how to show their concern, especially when it's someone at work, and *especially* when they don't really know what happened."

"I know."

"What did Kyle say?"

The woman was like an emotional bloodhound. "I didn't really tell him."

"Oh? Why?"

"I told him it sucked."

"But not why?"

"No."

"What did he say?"

I imitated Kyle with an emphatically stupid tone, "'Well, it's your first day back.'" Then I added, "As if you're supposed to run the gauntlet to get your entry badge back."

"Hmm."

"What?"

"I'm just worried about you."

"Me? Why?"

"Well, what you've been through is horrible. It may be the most horrible thing you'll ever go through."

"Let's hope."

"Agreed. But your co-workers don't know the truth about Kyle, and that turned out hard on you, and Kyle doesn't know the truth about your co-workers, and that was hard on you. I feel like you don't have a lot of people to support you who know the whole story. And that's not fair to you, or to them."

"And I feel like you are saying there are a lot of people I'm not telling the truth to!"

"Honey, I understand why you wouldn't want everyone to know. It's really not everyone's business."

"Exactly!"

"But it's also hard to keep that up. It takes energy. That's something you can run out of. You might feel better if you were just honest with everyone. No one is going to think less of you. No one who cares about you, anyway."

Under my breath, I mumbled, "Yeah, right."

"What's that?"

I sighed. "I said *I'm fine*. And my friends know."

"They do?"

"Yes, they are the ones who moved our apartment."

"I remember."

"And I have a couple of friends at work who know, too."

"That's good, I'm glad." She sounded resigned. The probe was over.

"I'm here at the apartment now, so I've gotta go."

"Are you sure?"

"Yes, I'll call you later."

"You know I love you. Call me any time."

"Okay, love you too, bye."

I hung up, then walked the last five blocks home.

I was on edge when I opened the door to the apartment and it did not help that I again heard the television on in the living room. I paused at the entryway bench to take off my shoes.

"You here?" I called.

"Yeah."

"My kingdom for a martini!"

"I thought you were going to the gym?"

"I did!"

"That wasn't long."

"At least I went."

"And the first thing you want afterwards is a martini?"

"No!" Dammit, *yes*. I was surly now, and I headed straight to the shower.

"Here." I heard him through the shower curtain and smiled as I saw him set a martini on the dresser outside the bathroom door. I quickly finished my shower and donned my fuzzy robe and towel head dress so I could scoop up my hard-won martini.

He was puttering around in the bedroom, apparently gathering clothes for a load of wash.

"Are you up for going out this weekend?" I delivered this in the form of a question but it was undeniably a statement of what we were going to do. I did not like being that girl, but I could not take another weekend of self-imposed exile with only the television for company, and after the martini "win" I was going to try to ride that wave of success as far as it would go.

He made a face. "Okay."

"Friday? We can try that tapas place?" I was ignoring everything but the agreement.

"Or we could order in and watch television?"

Now it was my turn to make a face. "We've been doing that for weeks."

"It's a lot cheaper that way."

"Only if you discount my lost sanity."

"Okay." He shrugged with maddening acceptance.

I kept my mouth shut. I had two wins.

The next day, my mom called but I let it go to voicemail. "Hi honey, I'm just checking in. Love you."

I went to the gym after work again, but I was in no hurry to get back to the apartment only to watch Kyle sit in front of a television—as surely was my fate—so I skipped the bus and walked home again, with a fair amount of dawdling on the way.

I was not far from home when I saw a good-looking man a little older than me walking toward me with a look of friendly recognition in his eyes. He looked familiar, but I could not place him. Shoot, where do I know him from?

"Hey!" he called cheerily.

"Hey!" I smiled back.

"It's great to see you. It's been awhile." He stopped opposite me and generously rescued me from my social floundering. "Ryan...I dated Kaia for a bit."

"Ryan! Oh, right! I'm sorry!" Kyle and I had really liked him, but our friend Kaia went through men like a kid goes through rides at the fair, and a few months later she had showed up with someone new. We had unseriously considered keeping him in the group instead of her.

"No problem," he grinned. "That was a couple of years ago now. Do you live around here?"

"Yes, a few streets over. We just moved in a couple of months ago. Do you remember my boyfriend, Kyle?"

"Yeah, great guy! He killed me in disc golf. Does he still play?"

"He hasn't played yet this season. He had a bit of an accident and he's still recovering, but I'm sure he'll be out there soon." I hesitated, knowing I had, without thinking, opened a weighty door with this conversation. Or maybe I had been thinking.

"Oh, man, I hope he's okay. What happened?"

I realized I wanted to tell him about it. And he did not hang around anyone I knew anymore so if I regretted it afterward it could be like this conversation never even happened.

I filled my lungs with air. "Actually..." And I went on to tell him everything about how I found him, the 911 call, the ambulance, and then I paused and looked at him to see how it landed.

His face was grave. "I'm sorry to hear that."

I believed him.

"How is he doing now?"

"Oh, better. He's getting his voice back and talking about going back to work."

"And what about you? I remember you guys had a pretty big group of friends. Are they helping you out?"

"He hasn't felt up to going out much yet, so Friday will be the first time we'll see them in quite a while."

He nodded. "I'm sure he's looking forward to it."

I forced some laughter. "No, not really. It took an act of Congress to get him out of the house last weekend. These days he'd rather just sit on the couch and watch sports." I held my breath, tilting my head down to look at the pitted sidewalk.

Ryan was quiet, and I raised my eyes and smiled—a real smile. After a moment, he dug in his back pocket for his wallet. "I know you have plenty of friends, but if there's anything I can do to help, don't hesitate to reach out." He offered me a business card.

I vainly tried to back up, laughing, waving off the proffered card. "Thank you, but he's better every day! He'll be back beating you at disc golf in no time!"

Ryan put his hand with the business card down by his side. "Look, it doesn't have to be me, but you should really make sure you have someone to talk to with all of this. Do you have someone?"

I lowered my eyes and quietly choked on my reality.

"Please." He offered me the card again, and I reached out and took it...

It was quite a bit later when I finally made it back to the apartment. I quietly opened the door, and with slow deliberation, I set my bag and the business card on the bench, took off and hung my coat, and slipped out of my shoes and lined them up against the wall. Everything in its proper place, everything except the business card on the bench.

I picked it up.

I walked into the living room behind where Kyle sat staring at the television. I fingered the business card, letting its sharp-ish corners dig into my fingertips. I stared at the television, too, trying to decipher its current spell over Kyle.

He turned around and smiled that stupid smile. "Hey, I didn't hear you come in."

I smiled back at him, not sure if it was from sarcasm or resignation (or maybe just animal mimicry), then walked into the kitchen.

"I ran into Ryan on the way home. Do you remember him? The guy Kaia was dating?"

"Yeah! I liked him!"

"Me too." I paused. "I didn't remember that he was a doctor."

"A doctor? Huh. I didn't remember that either."

I took one last look at the business card before dropping it into the drawer where things went to disappear forever.

Kyle's voice had been strengthening and his speech improved. It was not completely back, however, and I wondered if it ever would be. The ligature marks had faded a little, but exertion and emotion brought them back.

The next day, he talked about going back to work.

I was shocked.

He did not notice.

On my mental checklist of what order these things should happen, going back to work was considerably down the list from...other things...that I would have liked and expected to happen. We were young, we were healthy, and we should have been enjoying our twentysomething bodies. We had always been good that way, but that had not been in the air lately.

I picked up my phone to call my mom, and then set it down, staring at its darkened screen.

Instead, I wrote it on my list of questions.

Kyle and I went out for tapas that Friday, as promised. He even put some effort into dressing up. Or rather, I put some effort into dressing him up—in a new turtleneck I'd bought to match a pair of his pants that I liked—and he went along with it.

"You look great!" I said from across the table.

"Thanks. But you picked it out."

"Then I made you look great. You are welcome."

"I think these pants are too tight." He shifted in his seat, as if that would get rid of his newly acquired weight. It was not "these pants," it was all his pants.

Fortunately, at that moment, the waitress came up to give us menus, so I was saved from choosing between lying or truthing. I also had a bigger agenda for the evening and I did not want it to be derailed by a conversation we could have at home on any given night.

While we were both looking over the menu, I insinuated my idea. "Some people are going to Reiser's tonight for cocktails. I thought we could join them after dinner."

"Some people?"

"Sara and Alexander, Ann and a new girl she's dating. Maybe a few others."

"I don't know. I'm not sure I'm up for that."

"Come on, they want to see you! And we haven't gone out in forever."

Kyle was quiet and kept his eyes on his menu. After awhile, he said, "If you want to go."

I looked at him. "I would like to."

He did not say anything.

"Are you embarrassed? Is that why you don't want to see anyone?"

"No." His eyes told me I was introducing an uncomfortable new thought in his head. I was not sure where to go from there. I did not know what he was thinking. We had still never talked about what had happened.

"Well," I said, laying my napkin across my lap, "I would like to go."

"Okay."

There were more plates of food presented than words spoken throughout dinner that night. After the dishes had been cleared and the bill paid, we headed to Reiser's to catch up with our friends. Kyle held the front door open for me. I took his free hand in mine in what could have been mistaken for affection, but was really to make sure he followed me in. We stepped into the raucous dimness.

Just as expected, there were many more friends there than I had let on, all pressed up against the bar in some sort of individually synchronous unit that moved together, laughed together, and demanded to be fed a constant stream of cocktails together. The disparity between my estimate and the reality of the group that was there did not escape Kyle's attention.

"Geez, everyone is here."

I squeezed his hand in what I hoped was affection rather than control.

We were spotted immediately when we walked in. Four different voices shouted, "Kyle!" Our friends cloistered around him in wave after wave of smiles, hugs, and handshakes.

"I'm going to get us some drinks," I told him, half yelling and half signing.

I let myself drift to the edge of the group, where I could get the bartender's attention and watch the whole scene. It struck me that they congregated like gazelles— here for the good of the herd but nervous, ready to bolt. Fortunately, nothing had spooked them yet.

The bartender leaned toward me, shouting through the din, "What can I get you?"

"Two dry vodka martinis." He nodded, and I turned back to watch the crowd again. I was pleased to see Kyle smiling, laughing, and, well, engaging, considering his initial reaction to the idea at dinner. It was good to see.

Our friend Isaac emerged from the group, holding a protective hand in front of his cocktail since he was a little person and was in more danger than others of having his drink jostled free. He looked dapper, as always, in a navy suit. He hopped up on one of the barstools to get the bartender's attention, then he saw me. "Lauren!"

I smiled and moved over next to him, and he gave me a side-hug squeeze. "I'm glad you guys are here!"

"Me too!"

"I was about to get Kyle a drink. Did you already order?"

"Yeah, and I got one for Kyle."

"Put their drinks on my tab!" Isaac shouted through the revelry to the bartender, pointing at me. The bartender nodded and continued his work on our drinks.

"Aw, thanks, Isaac."

Then our friend Gabe strode over. "Lauren, love of my life!" Isaac rolled his eyes. Gabe was as full of insincere titillations as ever. He draped his arm over my shoulders and pulled me close. "You're not still dating Kyle, are you?"

I pushed him away, laughing and repulsed. "Of course."

He pulled me close again. "Leave him. We could be on the beach by the time the sun comes up tomorrow."

"That would be a crowded beach," Isaac said, sipping his cocktail. "Didn't you just give that same line to that girl at the table?"

"Judas!" Gabe released me.

"I'm just saying," Isaac continued. "At least stagger the times. Maybe sun*set* instead?"

But Gabe's head was already swiveling for the next woman to mount his arm around. "We'll never make headlines tonight if we're this subdued!"

"That's a relief," Isaac said.

Just then the bartender pushed two beautiful martinis across the bar to me. "Here you are."

"Thank you!" I said to the bartender, reaching for them. Then to Isaac, "I'm going to bring Kyle his drink."

I could only take so much of Gabe, and it was time to cut it short.

"I'll join you." Isaac, clearly of the same mind, hopped off his chair.

But we need not have run. Gabe was already eyeing a woman down the bar who was seated with her friend. "I'll catch up with you in a minute," he said, unbuttoning the top button of his shirt with a flourish. "Let the headlines begin." With that, he walked off toward his evening's destiny.

Isaac and I looked at each other, shaking our heads.

"Why are we friends with that guy again?" I said.

"Inertia," Isaac answered.

I laughed.

I took a sip from each extremely full martini glass, Isaac grabbed his drink from the bar, and we started to make our way through the throng back to Kyle.

Then I heard a soft voice behind me. "Lauren, hi."

I turned gently, mindful of the drinks in my hands, to see Ann standing there, camouflaged, as ever, in her quietness.

In the background, I could hear Gabe move in down the bar, saying "Ladies!" then a murmur too low to make out, then a burst of laughter from the two women. I secretly wished I knew what he had said that could pull that off.

I turned my full attention to Ann. "Hi, it's so good to see you!" It was not a lie. "Is your girlfriend here?" I wanted to meet the woman who had taken the time to unearth a jewel like Ann.

Behind me, I heard Isaac. "I'll meet you over there!" he said, pointing toward Kyle.

I turned back to Ann. Her mouth had only the subtlest of pulls at the edges, and that hint of a smile did nothing to negate the sadness in her eyes. "I asked her to get us drinks. I wanted to talk to you alone for a minute."

I stood up straight.

"I know about Kyle."

I looked at the ground. "Yeah, I figured everyone does."

"They do. But I don't think anyone will bring it up." She laid her hand lightly on my arm, and I looked up at her again. "But I wanted to tell you...it's a lot, what you're going through. I don't know exactly, but some of it. I had a brother..."

Ann stopped and swallowed hard. She looked down for a moment, and when she looked up again her eyes were shimmering. My chest felt like it had been filled with concrete.

"We were close. He was older than me. I was sixteen."

My mouth fell open slightly. Years had clearly done nothing to ameliorate it for her, and I was only months in.

"It took me a long time to realize it wasn't my fault, that it had nothing to do with me. I want to tell you it had nothing to do with you, either."

My mind raced. Kyle was still alive. We are going to be fine. But my sorrow for Ann overwhelmed me, and my chin trembled.

"I just want you to know that if you want to talk, I'm here. I don't know, really, what I can offer you, except ten years of experience."

Ten years. And there it was, just below the surface. My eyes ached with pressure from the tears trying to push through. I could not cry now. Not with two martinis in my hands.

At that moment, a woman I did not know approached with drinks, and Ann stopped talking. The woman looked my age, a year or so younger than Ann, with heavy eyebrows and long, light brown hair that was trying to curl at the ends. The woman grinned at Ann and offered her one of the cocktails. Ann smiled, a real smile this time, and thanked her.

The woman then turned to me. "Hi!"

Ann quickly introduced us. "Lauren, this is Dani. Dani, Lauren."

"Nice to meet you," Dani said. "Double-fisting?" She gestured at the martinis.

"Oh, no. I, uh, was just taking them to my boyfriend."

"Both of them? Wow, he's ready to get the party started!"

I laughed. I liked her already. "Seriously, though, I had better unload his before rumors get started."

"Okay, I never saw you," Dani said, looking away.

I laughed again, and Ann was smiling at her. I was happy for her.

"Come meet Kyle when you get a chance," I told Dani, nodding in the direction where we would be. I was already inching away.

"We will. We'll be over in a few minutes," Ann said.

I was still smiling when I wove my way through the group back to Kyle, Isaac, and the others.

"Still two martinis!" Isaac, perched on another stool, declared when he saw me, holding out his open hand to Brock, another friend in the circle.

"Oh man!" Brock said. "Lauren, be honest, did you go back and get another martini? There's money on the line here."

"Nope, these are the original goods." I laughed, handing one to Kyle.

Brock scowled and slapped a dollar into Isaac's waiting hand.

"Wait, what does that say about me? You actually *bet* that I couldn't walk twenty feet without downing a martini?"

"You took so long!" Brock protested.

Isaac interrupted, raising his glass. "To Kyle!"

Everyone in the circle roused and clinked their various glasses to each other and took a drink. Except Kyle, who chuckled, blushed, and looked down at his glass.

As I watched the group churn around us, I realized Ann was right. No one let on that they noticed his voice had not always been gravelly, or that he had never worn a turtleneck before. It was almost like nothing had happened: we were back hanging out with our friends like we had always done.

I looked up at him and it was Kyle—not Kyle the patient or Kyle the suicide risk. It was Kyle, my boyfriend.

Kyle caught me looking at him and laid his arm across my shoulders.

We stayed for about an hour and one more martini before he asked if I was ready to go. The glaze of alcohol added soft focus to the loving portrait I had framed of him that night. Still it ended just like every other recent night, with me falling asleep alone in our bed with only the cold glow of the television he was watching in the living room reaching me.

Kyle's next follow up appointment with Dr. Ehrlich was the following Monday, and I brought out the lists.

He turned to Kyle to respond to "our" questions. "Your voice should return fully in time. And if it doesn't keep improving, there are things we can try. Your stamina, too, will return. You didn't have any injuries that would prevent that."

Privately, after Kyle was sent to wait outside, with me, the doctor said, "His changes in personality could be the drugs. I can try something else to see if that makes a difference. As for the lack of sex drive, that could be related to the drugs as well. If he is ready to go back to work, I agree that it seems he would also be ready to return to the bedroom."

I smiled to myself at the doctor's "bedroom" euphemism for sex and wondered if that was to make me more comfortable, or himself.

Dr. Ehrlich jotted down a few notes and added, "I'll call in some new medications. Let's give it a couple-to-three weeks and see if there is any improvement in those areas."

"Thank you, doctor."

That week, I waited for something to change. Nothing seemed to, but I kept delaying my expectations with the rationale that it would take a while for the medications to have an effect.

One night, after going to the gym, and after seeing—and not returning—another call from my mom, I decided to stop by the store for some groceries and—the real reason for the trip—a bottle of wine. We had minimal cocktail ingredients at the apartment, but wine seemed more grown up and responsible. So I came home with it squirreled away in the bag and snuck it into the cocktail cabinet when I was unpacking.

"You went grocery shopping?" Kyle said from the couch when he saw me head for the kitchen as soon as I got home.

"Yeah, just picked up a few things."

"Are you going to cook something?"

I laughed. "No."

"Then what'd you get?"

"Just some chips and stuff."

"Oh."

I did not open the wine that night, or the next, or the next. But it was there.

We stayed home most nights—or every night—under the guise of "getting better," which, ironically, was making me feel worse. Added to that were the mounting number of calls and texts from my mom that I was leaving unanswered. We had not talked since the day after I returned to work, and I felt bad about how I had left it. Still, I did not call. It was the longest we had ever gone without talking. I told myself it was because I wanted to be able to share some good news when I talked to her, but the truth was some tangent off that.

Saturday was April Fool's Day, and while that was typically a nothing day for us, I was getting antsy to be more than a study of "two people in an apartment with a television," and it was coming out in less-than-helpful ways. After I proposed a series of activities that day, only to be shot down, I went for it.

"Do you want a glass of wine?"

"We have wine?"

"Yes, do you want some or not?"

He looked at me from the sanctity of the couch. "No thanks."

"Okay." I went to get my own glass, secretly happy I would not have to share.

He watched me get the bottle, get the glass, and pour myself the glass of wine. I took a very public sip, resenting his intrusion on my alcohol autonomy. Then, with all the obstinance in the world, I walked over and sat next to him on the couch, pretending to look at whatever stupid sports event he was watching.

He said nothing and turned his head back toward the television, but I could see him size up my glass out of the corner of his eye.

We sat for hours watching his sport of choice, while I followed up the first glass of wine with a second, then a third, and then finally the dregs of the bottle, without ever asking him again if he wanted some.

Slowly, as the wine gained purchase over me, the television annoyed me less and less, and I became absorbed in my own thoughts. This, I thought, was an easier way to pass the time. I slowly, gently, lowered myself into the couch and let it cradle me. When I opened my eyes again, the outside and the television were both dark, and Kyle's couch divot was empty. He must have made his way to the bedroom.

I was content to stay on the couch that night.

The next morning, I awoke late. Kyle was already up and watching the television in bed. He had been doing that a lot lately. I hated television in the morning. Especially in bed. I was not a big fan anyway, but in the morning the onslaught of flashing eye candy and blaring messages was exceptionally assaulting to me.

Caffeine is Priority One. I would have that printed on a t-shirt, I thought as I pushed myself up from the couch.

"Do you want coffee?" I called to him.

He appeared in the bedroom doorway, still unable to stretch his voice far enough to respond from the bed. "No, I'm good. So, are you up?"

"If you want to call it that."

I shuffled into the kitchen to the appliance that was the giver of semi-fancy coffee drinks, and hit the user-friendly combination of buttons that delivered the magic. "User-friendly" before caffeine must be a whole, separate level of user-friendliness, I thought as I stared at the machine while it performed.

Coffee in hand, I shuffled back into the living room where Kyle was firmly planted in front of what he now referred to as "the good TV." I sat down next to—and possibly slightly on—him.

He grunted, smiled, and shifted over.

With half-closed eyes, I embraced my oversized cup, both for its warmth and the possibly questionable promises it made for improved sharpness and long life. Mmm, promises. For a while the television held all the conversations by itself, but as the coffee started to take hold, I felt like I wanted to play an active part.

"I think I'll go to the gym this morning. Want to come?"

"Not sure I'm feeling up to it yet."

I reached over and poked his newly-squishy midsection and gave him a look full of earnest meaning. "So apparently it's not a *weight* you're working up to before you go, because I think you're *there* on that front."

"Hey!" he objected and grabbed my poking finger, laughing.

A minor tussle ensued, but when he hesitated after I howled a protest about being roughhoused while holding hot coffee, I gained the upper hand and sat atop him triumphantly. "Sucka!" After which I was instantly toppled, coffee be damned.

I sat up from the floor, a dashing new coffee-colored racing stripe across my jammie top. I winced, holding the hot, wet shirt away from my skin. "I deserved that."

I was taken aback by the horrified look on his face. He jumped down to pick me up, stammering apologies. "I'm sorry! I'm sorry! I shouldn't have done that!"

"It's okay! We were just playing!" Like we have done a million times before.

He continued to apologize and looked like he was near tears, ineffectually wiping the coffee stain with a napkin left over from a previous night's dinner.

"Hey!" I grabbed his hand to stop him. "It's *okay*. Stop."

He stared at me, trembling. He looked so piteous I had to hug him so he did not see the complete confusion on my face. What the hell was this?

For the rest of the day, Kyle's reaction to the coffee incident bothered me. I did not feel like I needed to tell the doctor about it because it was just a weird moment, and I did not want the doctor to see it as anything more than that. Everything else was going well. I decided I just needed to give Kyle, and the new medications, more time.

The next morning at work, I was uncharacter-istically on time, but characteristically not focused on work. I was already planning my workout at the gym afterward, and maybe I would stop for a drink somewhere on the way home?

Shortly into my daydreams, Megan sauntered into my cubicle and asked if I wanted to go to lunch with her and Hannah. I paused, unintentionally, but long enough for her brow to furrow an accusation.

"You don't *have* to."

Clearly I *did* have to. "Yeah, totally!"

"We'll come get you around 12:30?"

"Okay."

Megan walked away, glancing back at me as she did. I turned back to my computer, chagrinned.

Megan and Hannah: There was no way of putting the lid back on that box. I had called them forth, and now they were going to stay *forth*. To do anything else was to chance having the entire office know every sordid detail of what had happened with Kyle.

I groaned and returned to my work.

As promised, Megan and Hannah came by to collect me for lunch. I smiled and grabbed my purse, determined to keep them on my side.

"Let's go to The Sidewinder," Megan proposed once we were out of the building.

"The Sidewinder! Are they even open right now?" I asked.

The Sidewinder was a small, dingy bar about ten minutes away that fronted a very busy road. The three of us had been there for a drink after work a time or two. Hannah and I liked the irony of being young women dressed for work in a place like that. For some reason, Megan just like-liked it.

"Eww," said Hannah. "Do they even have food?"

"They open at 8 AM. And they have a full menu."

"8 AM? You're kidding. Who is going there at 8 AM?" I said.

"People who work the night shift? People they kicked out at closing the night before?" Megan had already started walking in that direction. "They have a breakfast and beer special."

"I do like their margaritas," Hannah said, falling in line behind Megan. Apparently, Hannah was on board.

Sure enough, I could see The Sidewinder's neon *Open* sign flickering as we approached.

"I don't even want to know how you knew about the breakfast special," I said to Megan.

She gestured at a sign in front of the bar's almost invisible door that advertised eggs, bacon and toast with a pitcher of beer for a price almost anyone could afford. "My bus drives right by it every morning."

Hannah stopped to read the sign. "A whole pitcher?!"

I shook my head and Megan pulled open the door. We stepped into the black void inside, practically stepping on each other as we paused and waited for our eyesight to return.

There were a handful of men in the bar—one playing the lottery, one playing pool by himself, and two sitting at the bar, plus the one tending it. The men watched as the three of us bumbled uncomfortably over to a table not too far from the door and settled in.

The bartender, who I was sure was in a band that never got gigs, shuffled over with a pitcher of water, a stack of plastic water glasses, and food-splattered menus. He took our drink order and said he would be right back to take our food order.

"Maybe I'll just get a salad," Hannah said, looking at the menu.

Megan, also looking at the menu, clicked her tongue. "I think your best play here is getting something that started frozen and was then submerged in boiling oil."

We ordered and the food came, piled high to the point of being barely contained by the plates it came on. I was suspicious that quantity was trying to make up for quality, but after sampling it, I hated to admit the food was not bad. Still, this was not the plan. What

I *wanted* to be doing that lunch hour was maybe some clothes shopping. What I *was* doing was sitting in an authentically old, dirty bar with Megan and Hannah, eating more than I wanted to eat, spending more than I wanted to spend, and day-drinking because they had glared at me like I had killed music when I had tried to order an iced tea after they had ordered drinks.

"So..." Megan took a long drag of her second margarita. "I heard from my cousin yesterday. He's going to be in town in a couple of weeks for work. I thought maybe the three of us could meet up with him one night for dinner and drinks?"

"Is he cute?" Hannah asked.

Megan ignored her. "He has a bunch of work stuff going on, so I'm not sure what night yet."

"Yeah, sure," I said, with no real thought about it, other than keeping her on my side.

"I bet he'll pick up the bill, too. He has a great job."

"Cool."

"Ooh!" Hannah leaned forward. "Let's go somewhere nice then!"

"Maybe. I'll see." Megan pushed her plate away. "Are you guys ready to head back?"

Hannah took this as her cue to finish her margarita, and I took it as the chance to not finish mine. We paid the bill and stepped outside to be blinded once again.

The walk back to the office included a heated debate about whether to issue a general endorsement of The Sidewinder as a lunch option, the proposal of which earned one "yay" (Megan), one "nay" (Me), and an expression of approval for their margaritas (Hannah).

"Why do you like their margaritas so much?" I asked Hannah. "They're nothing special. They're made with mixer. Not even a good mixer."

"I like mixer. It's nice and sweet without being too limey."

"But margaritas are all about the lime! How can you say you don't like the lime when that is the main flavor?"

"Then I guess I like whatever drink tastes like mixer."

"A Floor Cleaner-ita?" Megan offered.

"A Cloytini? A Chemicalipolitan?" I added. "It's like a Pinto."

"Pinto?" Megan stopped and turned to me, brow wrinkled.

"Basically the opposite of a Cadillac."

"Ah, the car. I was thinking the bean." We continued walking.

Hannah was grumpy now. "You don't have to like it." We walked on and she added, "I don't get the 'Koitini.' Isn't that a fish?"

"Not koi, 'cloy.'" I said.

"I don't know what that is."

"It's when something is sickeningly sweet."

In response, Hannah resorted to a poor parody of me, with her version of someone posh walking with a martini and a pinky in the air. "I'm Lauren and I drink martinis. And I went to a fancy college so I could learn words like 'cloy.'"

"Facts," Megan said. She was not helping.

We were almost back at work so we tabled the cocktail discussion and passed around mints.

"I'll let you guys know about dinner," Megan said.

"What dinner?" I asked.

"With my cousin?"

I made a face that said I had already forgotten about that. She rolled her eyes and flung open the front door, marching through it.

In the weeks since his medication change, I thought I could see a subtle change in Kyle. I was not sure how, but maybe he was a bit more engaged? Maybe he had more energy? Or maybe it was just my imagination. The consistent thread was "maybe."

Kyle had continued seeing the therapist, though less frequently. He never brought it up with me, even though so much of our life right now was centered around it. I never brought it up either. The closest I would get was to sometimes ask how his therapy went. The usual answer was "fine," so it was a safe question.

However, that week, when I asked how his therapy went, he said the therapist had asked him for details about the events leading up to that day and anything he remembered about it.

"Wow." I paused, then added, "What did you say?"

Kyle looked at me with a look I thought was pregnant with meaning, but then he shrugged. "I don't remember much. It's all pretty foggy."

"Foggy."

"Yeah."

I was silent. *My* memory of the event was as clear as if I was carrying around a *National Geographic* pictorial on it. No one ever throws those away, but somehow, he had been able to.

That Saturday, I went to the gym early, then returned to the apartment with the great idea of going to the farmers market in the next neighborhood. Kyle did not share my enthusiasm.

"What are we going to get at a farmers market? We don't cook." Kyle said from the couch. "Besides, it's raining."

"Lightly misting. They have a lot of stuff besides vegetables. Cheese and fruit and stuff." I went to the bedroom to shower in preparation for going to the market.

"Fruit? It's barely spring," he said, still on the couch.

I was undeterred. "Come on, it'll be fun."

"There's a game on I want to watch."

"Save it. Watch it later."

I waited, but did not hear a response. I peeked out the door of the bedroom and saw him still on the couch, so I sweetened the deal. "We can stop for good coffee on the way." It was not a totally selfless proposition: I had forgotten to get some earlier and my head was bursting with desire for caffeine.

Kyle's head swiveled my direction, and I could see the resignation on his face. "Fine."

He heaved himself up with some significant groaning and trudged into the bedroom with all the enthusiasm of a kid going to test day at school.

"How long do you think we'll be there?" He was standing, shoulders drooped, in front of his side of the closet like he was waiting for the clothes to fly out and dress him, a la Cinderella.

Now I was getting exasperated. "I don't know! Can't we just have fun with it?" I pulled a sweater from my drawer and threw it on the bed.

"I was having fun," he said quietly.

"Forget it! I'll go by myself." I threw some pants down with gusto and tromped into the bathroom to shower.

He followed me to the doorway. "You're mad."

I turned on the water and turned around to look at him. "Yes, I am mad! We never do anything anymore, and when I try to get you to do something, all you do is complain."

He looked at the floor.

"You used to be up for anything," I went on.

Kyle turned away without looking up, and I turned back to my shower.

When I came out of the bedroom twenty minutes later, yes, he was watching television again, but he was also dressed for the market.

"Does that mean you're coming with me?"

"Yes." He switched off the television and stood up with his coat.

Jointly, if not together, we silently put our shoes on.

We stopped at the first coffee shop we saw on the way to the farmers market, just two blocks away from our apartment. It was an appealing, local shop, refreshingly far on the spectrum from the perfectly staged national chain that had been ubiquitous in our last neighborhood.

There were quite a few people in line, but the heady smell of the roasted beans was a siren song to my aching caffeine dependency, so we stayed.

The menu boards were all hand-lettered, with the previous lettering not totally erased, and they boasted of items they assumed you would know: *Maggie's Muffins* and *New Day Kombucha*. None of the tables or chairs seemed to match, or if they did, great care had been taken in locating them so you would never know. The walls displayed the work of different local artists—some excellent, and some...working on their craft.

A couple about our age was in line ahead of us. They were looking at a flyer on the shop's community posting board for a local bike ride event that was "clothing optional."

I overheard the man say to the woman, "Look at that flyer. A naked bike ride to protest oil dependency!"

I chuckled. I had known about the event for several years since I moved to the city—I had even caught a glimpse of it before by accident—but it still made me giggle like a fifth grader to think about it.

Kyle could not figure out what I was doing. I tried to communicate it telepathically and through a series of head nods, eyebrow raises, and intense glances, but somehow it did not work.

"What? What are you doing?" he said, confounded.

I rolled my eyes at him for outing me so loudly and waved him off so I could keep listening.

The woman scrutinized the flyer. "Yikes. Don't loan anyone your bike that weekend."

"What about the rental bikes? I doubt they have a formal cleaning program for those."

I tried to stifle my laugh but somehow that just amplified it.

The woman turned around, blushing furiously. "I'm sorry! We were just..." She thumbed in the direction of the flyer. "We don't have stuff like that where we come from."

I laughed openly now. "Trust me, I get it. There are lots of considerations—sun protection, chafing, seat style..."

"Have you done it?" She gawked.

"No. But now that you mention it..." I pulled out my phone like I was going to get a picture and save the date.

We all three laughed and Kyle looked like he did not understand why I was laughing with strangers. I tried to explain. "They saw the flyer for the Naked Bike Ride."

Somehow that did not help, and Kyle stood looking at me, unhappy and confused. I did not have the energy to push through that dense wall, so I went back to chatting with the couple.

The line was dispatched quickly by the cheerfully efficient baristas, and in no time at all, we had chatted our way to the front of the line. We continued talking while waiting for everyone's coffee, and by the time we were picking tables to sit down, we were so engrossed in conversation, we three just naturally walked to a table together.

Kyle was quiet and, upon joining us at the table, I realized he was sullen. I was not sure I had ever seen him sullen before. The couple had noticed Kyle was not joining in, but after trying to draw him out with some questions about himself and getting very little response, they seemed to accept it at face value.

I did not care. I was having a genuinely good time, and I wanted to enjoy it. If he wanted to be like that, I was not going to let it get in the way of my fun.

We stayed well after we finished our coffees, and when we finally left for the market, they came with us under the guise of being new to the area and wanting to find out where it was.

By early afternoon, after hours of eyeing and tasting our way around the booths, and with both guys laden with bags of impulse buys, we were ready to commit to something more serious than the cheese and produce samples that had awakened our stomachs.

"How about finding some lunch nearby?" our new friends suggested.

Kyle jumped in before anyone could respond, "No, we can't. We have to go home." Then he turned to me. "Come on Lauren, let's go."

That was it. No discussion, no discreet exchange of looks to determine where we stood on the matter, not even a fake excuse to explain the rejection. Just *no*.

It stopped us all in our tracks, and I quickly asked for her contact information and begged for a rain check as the weakest of covers.

I was fuming as we walked down the block away from the market and away from the disappointed couple. "What was that about? Why didn't you want to get some lunch with them?"

"I don't know, I just didn't."

"You weren't even nice about it! I was totally embarrassed."

"Let's just go home." He reached out for my arm, but I neatly sidestepped his grasp.

"YOU go home. I'm not going to just sit at home watching television all night every night." I started walking in the opposite direction. I did not know where I was going but I knew I needed a break from him.

"Wait!" Kyle turned around after me and grabbed my arm, holding me fast. "Where are you going?"

"I don't know!" I was shocked he would lay his hand on me like this. His touch was unwelcome and I was not going to suffer it in silence. I yanked free of his control and glared at him. "Don't touch me!"

His face got red and suddenly it occurred to me that we were perhaps now playing by new and different rules. But my fury had its foot on the neck of my better judgment, and I did not know how to back down.

We stared at each other. I braced myself.

He turned and walked away with a trail of red-hot temper in his wake, still holding the produce-stuffed bag from the market.

I exhaled in relief, then trembled with remembered anger. I watched him until he was blocks away, expecting him to throw down the bag in anger, but he never did.

I finally turned away and walked slowly down the city blocks, trying to figure out what to do that would keep me away for more time than he thought I would stay away for, but not so long that I would have to make an uncomfortable choice to do it. I wanted to unload part of this burden. I wanted to be told, with great sympathy, that Kyle was wrong and I was wronged.

I wanted to call my mom, but did not.

Eventually, I messaged Megan.

What are you doing?

Finishing up some errands. You?

Went to farmers market. Done now.

Want to meet for coffee in half an hour?

Yes.

She texted me the place. I could make it on foot but I had to hustle. But any day with Megan was a high-calorie day, so I could use the exercise.

The route took me through a touristy part of town that I did not often get to, even though it was a beautiful part of the city. I smiled, a little jealous of the exuberant hatted tourists, following maps and tour guides from sign to sign, place to place. I did not remember ever getting to be a tourist here, even though I grew up only a few hours north and went to school not that many train stops outside the city. Is it too late to be one?

As I neared the coffee shop, I saw Megan half a block ahead of me, and I trotted to catch up with her. "Megan!"

She glanced around, then nodded an acknowledgement and started walking back toward me.

"Good timing," she said as I walked up.

"Yeah," I said, a little out of breath.

We walked back toward the coffee shop together.

"So, you went to the farmers market?"

"Yeah."

"By yourself?"

"No, Kyle went with me, but we had a big fight and I don't want to go home."

"Ahh."

"What?"

"That makes more sense."

"What does?"

"It sounded fishy before, that you were hitting me up to do something on a Saturday afternoon."

I accepted the judgment with a regretful nod. It did sound fishy.

Then, as she failed to turn in the doorway of the coffee shop, Megan said, "There's a bar a few blocks from here that I want to try. Let's go there instead."

I agreed. Getting a coffee was not really what I wanted. I would save my adulting for another time.

Also without pretense, Megan didn't wait for our drinks to arrive before she said, "So, what happened?"

That was all the prompting I needed to launch into the story of my day, with all my indignities inflamed. I paused when I got to the part where he grabbed my arm, eager for her take.

"You're lucky it wasn't worse," she said. "I don't know how you can still be with him."

Well, that seems excessive. I mean, people argue...

But she was already off and planning what we were going to do that night.

"Oh, I don't know how much longer I'm going to stay out," I said.

She looked at me as if this scenario was covered in Dating 101. "You're going to stay out until it's time to go to sleep."

"What? No!"

"Yes. You're not going to sleep somewhere else, because that is crossing a line, and because I don't want you sleeping on my couch. But you are going to go out and have a good time until then. A very good time."

"I'm not going to a strip joint," I said, seriously.

"What? Eww! No."

"You never know with you!"

Megan nodded. "I can see that."

I did not open the door to my apartment again until what could only fairly be called early the next morning, well after last call. A lot had happened.

Kyle was, of course, sleeping when I arrived. Neither the light from the hallway nor my struggles shedding clothes disturbed him. He woke up only when I fell roughly down on my side of the bed and exhaled hugely, as if "sleeping" was the newest yoga pose.

"Where have you been?"

"With Megan."

"Megan from work?"

I sighed deeply to emphasize that this was now the time for sleep. "Yes."

"Since when did you start hanging out with her?"

Did he not hear the sigh? "I've hung out with her!" Good. Testy enough to hopefully end this questioning but also firm enough to attest to the truth of what I was saying.

"I tried calling you a bunch of times. I was worried."

"We were out. It was loud. I wasn't checking my phone." After a moment of no response, I thought he had gone back to sleep and was quickly following suit. But then I heard him roll away from me and realized he had been looking at me all that time. What was he thinking about?

I exhaled again. Nothing he had said or done in months made me think he was thinking about anything. And certainly not about me.

The curtains were quickly losing their battle to the growing daylight and I worried I would not be able to get to sleep, but that was my last thought before I was out, asleep, for most of the day.

Later that day, still in bed, the unseasonable heat was causing my hair to stick to my sweating face, and my campaign to keep it out of my mouth was a failure. I laid there, straining to hear where Kyle was in the apartment. It was hard to hear over the sound of the blood pulsating around my tender head, but surprisingly, I did not hear the television. I rolled partway over just to confirm that he was not still sleeping next to me, and no, there was only the indent where he had been.

I pulled on my pajamas and did my customary pre-caffeine shuffle out to the living room. Only his used coffee cup was there. I went to the kitchen under the auspices of starting my coffee. Not there either. Was he trying to get back at me for yesterday?

My coffee burbled its completion and I smiled as I cupped it and carried it to the living room. I was quietly sipping and scanning through the news of the day when I heard Kyle's key in the door. I was disappointed he was returning home so soon.

"Hey," I said with only the slightest turn of my head.

"Hey." He was holding a bag of groceries: mystery solved.

He walked past me into the kitchen. Apparently, we were not talking about yesterday's unpleasantness.

In the kitchen, he rustled his way around the shopping bag, slamming cabinets unabated. I pushed on my aching temples and cursed quietly to myself.

He wandered almost aimlessly back into the living room, armed—uncharacteristically—with an open bag of chips that was crinkling incessantly. He dropped into his customary spot on the couch and pointed the remote at the TV to bring it to life, ending any hope I had of a quiet cup of coffee.

I frowned into my cup. And at the couch. Stupid couch. I hate the couch. I scowled, almost evenly at the couch and him.

"When are we going to get a new couch?"

He looked at the couch. "New couch? Why?"

"I hate this couch. I've always hated this couch, you know that."

"You hate the couch?"

"I've *told* you that!" Maybe.

We sat in a sudden whirlpool of emotion, wondering where we—I, he, and the couch—go from here now that this dissatisfaction had been expressed in no uncertain terms.

"What's wrong with the couch?"

"I hate it!"

I stormed into the bedroom and slammed the door, much to the grimacing chagrin of my head. I was confused about what I had just done, which meant I could only imagine how confused he was.

Great, so now I am in the bedroom, I thought. Now what?

I crawled under the sheet and waited for my head to come to equilibrium without the cup of coffee it so craved. To my surprise, when I opened my eyes again, it was an hour later. I was perspiring again under the sheet and my head was still not on board with the idea of nothing being that bad. I kicked the sheet off and closed my eyes, hoping to sleep through the rest of the discomfort, but blessed sleep did not come, and the more I chased it, the more it evaded me. I laid there, wretched, sweating. I would have to make my own way through the discomfort.

It was dark when I finally opened the door to the bedroom again. I knew what I was going to see before I opened the door, so the only thing left to do was face it: Kyle, the couch, and the television in their happy polyamory. I was not in the mix.

But once it was there in front of me, feeling old and new at the same time, I realized I did not have the energy to face it. I turned and went back to the bedroom, and Kyle never noticed.

"So, was he mad?" Megan looped her arm over my cubicle half wall at work on Monday.

"No, he was asleep." I continued to type on my keyboard.

"He could have been both."

"He could have, but he wasn't. I would describe it more as curious, rather than anything that had an intimate emotion attached to it."

"Hot."

"Although...I guess..." I stopped typing and looked up, then leaned back in my ergonomically questionable chair.

"What?!" Megan asked, ready for some intrigue.

I looked at her. "Curiosity could be an intimate emotion, couldn't it?"

She snorted and walked away.

"I just want to be precise!" I said after her.

That day I was scheduled to call Dr. Ehrlich's office and let the nurse know how I thought the new medications were working.

"There is a small difference. I guess he seems a little better?"

"And have you resumed sexual activity?" Wow, she did not trouble herself with euphemisms.

"Erm, no."

"Have you tried initiating it?"

"No, should I? I mean...I guess I thought I should wait until he did it, in case..."

"He's medically strong enough for sex, if that's what you're wondering."

"Oh, okay."

"He should be fine for any physical activities he could do before. So, I would just go ahead and try that."

"Okay, great."

Because the nurse was encouraging, that night with Kyle I was encouraging. It ended with me angry and sleeping on the couch, and him, confused, watching television in our bed. I peevishly helped myself to what I had been looking for, then guiltily vowed to be more understanding with him.

Kyle went back to work the next week, with the doctor's blessing. He did programming and some project management for a large company, so the job wasn't physical and he probably could have gone back before he did. The afternoon of his first day back he let me know he would be home late because his coworkers wanted to take him out for a beer. It sounded like his first day back was going a lot better than mine had.

He apologized for not inviting me, but said it was just work people. Normally I would have had to hide my disappointment at not being included—I thought I got along great with the guys he worked with, and I loved the extra attention they gave me for being one of the few girls that hung around with their group—but today it was welcome news and I hoped they stayed out late, even though I knew they would not.

What would I do with my expectation-free night? Something Kyle would not want to do, which these days was just about everything.

I spent the next hour at work looking at restaurant reviews and keeping an eye out for my boss, Jim, who would surely prefer I do some actual work.

I settled on going to a sleek new place a few streets over from our apartment. We had walked by it in our wanderings, and I had wanted to try it, but Kyle thought it looked too pretentious. Perfect.

After work, I soared through my workout. At home, I changed outfits three or four times before settling on an edgy outfit of pieces I had never put together before. Between the new look, and dropping the pounds I had put on during Kyle's recuperation, I was feeling good.

I practically floated down the stairs of our building on anticipation alone. It was a warm night, with none of the chill of spring loitering.

To someone on the street, my hurry to get to there and hit "start" on my night of freedom must have made me look like the most confident woman in the world. In a way, I was. I was exactly who I wanted to be that night, going exactly where I wanted to go, doing only what I wanted to do.

Why don't I remember feeling like this before I met Kyle? All I remember is hoping there would be single guys wherever I was going. And probably, secretly, I went places where I thought they would be. But that was a long time ago now.

I rounded the final corner and could see a crowd of people already waiting outside the restaurant. I queued up to check in, flinching with awareness that I appeared to be the only one there by myself. Fortunately, not the only one who looked like me, which always gave me a tingle of additional ease. When the sea of people in front of me finally parted, the woman who was directing the seating smiled a greeting at me. I was up.

I stepped forward and lowered my voice. "One, please."

"Wonderful," she said, as if anything else would have been strange. "If you are okay sitting at the bar, I can seat you right away."

"Oh!" I felt chosen. "Yes, thank you."

She compiled the various menus I would need to make my decisions, and pushed open the huge metal-trimmed door to the restaurant. "Follow me."

I smiled as I walked after her, ignoring the frowns of the more impatient people left behind on the sidewalk.

Inside, the cavernous space was loud and crowded with people but sparsely decorated. A huge collection of dim lights clustered in the middle like a swirl of fish escaping whales. Kyle would hate this, I thought happily.

The bar was a huge glassy expanse of stone in the middle of the space. The girl spread out the menus, and pulled out the plush, high-backed stool for me. With another smile, she invited me to sit.

"Thank you!" I was not sure she could hear me over the din, but she nodded and smiled again before slipping back to her outpost.

"Hi." I turned to see the man greeting me from behind the bar with suspenders and the sleeves to his white shirt rolled up; I felt I had been transported to the origin of the cocktail. "Can I get anything started for you?"

"Oh, yes, a vodka martini please, very dry."

"You got it. Any preference on the vodka?"

Ordering it dry had always been my way of letting the bartender know to do his best because I was a woman who knew her martinis. But this bartender had taken it a step further. I felt like I had been found out. "Whatever you recommend."

He smiled at me like we shared a secret. "You got it."

I watched as the bartender poured and swirled the vodka, then waved the bottle of vermouth over the preparation, but without a drop hitting the drink. After a couple more flourishes with a twist of lemon peel, he set the glass in front of me, clearly confident this would be the best martini I had ever had. And it was.

I smiled deeply, eyes bright, and he nodded and smiled and said, "I'll give you a minute to look over the menu."

I nodded, still smiling.

Looking over the food menu was another thrilling wave of declaring myself—vegetables, vegetables, vegetables. Yes, maybe I would become a vegetarian, I thought. I convinced myself *Kyle* was the one who always wanted to get the meat dishes. I could totally be a vegetarian.

I revisited that idea after the plates had been swept away and I was still hungry and maybe a tiny bit unsatisfied. Okay, I might not be a vegetarian, but if not, it was because *I* did not want to be!

When the bartender came by again, I gestured toward my nearly empty martini glass. "Can I get another one of these when you get a chance?"

"Have you tried a gin martini?"

"No, should I?"

"Let me make you one. If you don't like it, I'll make you a vodka martini instead."

"Okay." I was excited.

He took a moment to choose a bottle from the gin section behind the bar, then repeated his magic. This time he deposited a splash of vermouth into the mixing pitcher as well.

I was skeptical about the vermouth, but when I tried the new variation, I was sold.

"Well?" he said after I took my first sip.

"Wow. That is delicious! I wasn't sure about the vermouth, but that is so good!"

"Great! Yeah, I really like the combination of a very botanical gin with just a hint of vermouth."

I nodded wide-eyed agreement at a description I barely understood. "Thank you so much!"

I realized I might be missing out on a lot by sticking with my standard martini order everywhere we went. For my third drink, I asked him to make me something else entirely, and once again, I was amazed.

After the third drink, I knew it was the perfect time to leave with perfect memories and to be remembered perfectly. I tipped generously and made a gracious exit, complimenting the bartender and assuring the hostess of an excellent experience, at which they both seemed genuinely pleased.

Based on the final price tag I realized that experience had to be something special, rather than routine. I stopped by a cheap local bar for a final cap on the night and replayed the events and revelations of the evening.

When my final drink was nearing the bottom and I knew it was time to head back to the apartment, I stared intently into the bottom of the cocktail glass, looking for the answers to my unarticulated questions, but could not make sense of them. So I left the answers in the bottom of the glass and made my way home.

When I opened the door, Kyle was already there in front of the television. I felt myself sink.

He turned, smiled, and looked at me. "Hey, where have you been?"

That stupid smile.

I turned toward the wall, peeling off my impossibly fantastic jacket to throw it on the bench, and kicking off my new favorite shoes.

"You're dressed up. Where did you go?" he repeated.

"Just grabbed some dinner by myself."

"Where at?"

"At that restaurant a few blocks over. The one you thought looked pretentious." I wobbled to the kitchen to get a glass of wine.

"By yourself?" His head turned to follow me into the kitchen. I knew he was wondering why I did not go out with friends, but I wanted to believe he was jealous and asking if I was really by myself and not with some other man, looking the way I did.

I poured my wine, in no hurry to respond. "Yes," then added, "I'm going to read in bed."

I did not want to give him the details of my night; I wanted them to be all mine. I did not wait for his response before I retreated to the bedroom to enjoy the fading residue of tonight's adventures. Curled up in bed with my wine next to me on the bedside table, I held my book open for appearances but just stared at the page, instead smiling at my night.

That night, I slept so well not even my dreams interrupted me.

•

When I came home from work and the gym the next day, I could hear Kyle talking to someone on the phone in the living room. I slipped out of my shoes, dropped my purse, and walked in behind him, trying to figure out who he was talking to.

Whomever it was, they were laughing and sharing a lot of "remember when" stories.

I went to the kitchen to pour myself a glass of wine from the bottle I had opened the previous day, then busied myself looking through the mail on the counter. Soon Kyle was saying goodbye with promises of not letting it be so long next time. He disconnected and looked at me with a goofy grin on his face. "That was a guy I played football with in high school."

"Crazy. He called you out of the blue?"

"No, Mom ran into him and his wife at the grocery store and she said I should call him."

"You talked to your mom today?"

"Yeah, she's been calling to check in."

"Oh." Strange that he would not mention that. "So he still lives there?"

"Yeah, he was a year ahead of me, but he married a girl in my class and they bought a house in the same neighborhood he grew up in, near his parents. It sounded really nice."

I shuddered audibly, and he looked at me, puzzled.

I tried to jog his memory. "Remember how we always said we were glad we didn't live near our parents?"

"Oh," he said, and turned the television on.

I resented being left alone in that joke, our joke, and headed for the bedroom with my wine.

Before I could get there, Kyle said, "Hey, what do you want to do for dinner?"

"I don't know. Whatever." I continued toward the bedroom, adding, "By the way I'm going out to dinner with Megan and her cousin tomorrow night."

"You hang out with Megan a lot now."

"Sometimes." I was in the bedroom now, doffing my gym clothes.

"Chinese?" Kyle called after me.

"Where from?"

"I don't care. Great Wall?"

I walked back into the living room, nose wrinkled.

He sighed when he saw me. "What do you want?" My little game of "Guess What Lauren Wants for Dinner" was clearly wearing on him.

"How about Dumpling House?" Adding, unnecessarily, "I love their dumplings."

"Okay."

We negotiated our dishes with each other, and Kyle, because he was the one who brought it up and that was our arrangement, placed the order.

Apparently with food still on the brain, Kyle returned to the previous topic. "Where are you going for dinner tomorrow?"

I was flipping through a catalog that had just arrived. "Somewhere downtown."

"Why downtown?"

I shrugged, but kept flipping. "I think that's where he's staying."

"Oh, it's a 'he'?"

"Apparently."

A few minutes later, after my interest in the catalog had waned, I looked up and caught Kyle turning away back toward the television.

"What?" I asked.

"Nothing."

We were set to meet Megan's cousin on Wednesday night. All I knew about him is that he was in computer engineering, kind of like Kyle, but in hardware instead of software. He was staying near his work downtown, so we all met at a swanky place near there.

The restaurant was old-school nice, with a classic neon sign and tuxedoed staff out front. I was the last to arrive because I had squeezed in a workout, even though Megan told me not to. And she had just texted me to let me know they were waiting to order food until I got there—as if I were an hour late, instead of twenty minutes!

But when I got inside, they were still sitting in the half-empty bar having pre-dinner cocktails—they had not even been seated yet. I raised questioning hands and eyebrows at Megan, but she just smirked and sipped her drink.

"This is my cousin John." She gestured at the fairly attractive man sitting next to her, who was probably in his mid-thirties and taller than I had expected, given that Megan was on the short side. Other than that, you could see a family resemblance. It was obvious in the almost-black hair and light skin, but there was also something in the face, especially the eyes. I realized I was analyzing it too much when he smiled at me and held a hand up in greeting.

"Hi," then I gestured to myself, "Lauren," and took the last remaining seat at the tall table, across from Megan and next to Hannah.

"So where are you from?" I asked John as I took my seat, feeling it was my duty as the tardy one to lead the charge back into sociability.

"Denver," Hannah answered, smiling at John, who I felt was instead still smiling at me.

I rolled my eyes. "Sorry I was late. I missed the introductions."

John waved it off. "We're not punching a clock. I'm glad we could do this."

The waiter approached the table. "Ah, our fourth has arrived."

I sighed.

"Your table is ready if you would like to be seated."

"Yes, thank you." John stood up to follow him, and Megan, Hannah and I all began gathering our belongings and drinks.

"We are happy to bring those to your table for you," the waiter gently counseled.

We exchanged sheepish looks. "Thank you," Megan said.

We trailed the waiter into an adjoining space that appeared to have been a separate storefront at some point before a doorway was punched through the common wall. The dining room was lovely, with chandeliers and luxurious draperies that hung from the top of the vaulted ceilings all the way to the floor.

Hannah was impressed and let a low "wow" escape.

As we all settled in to the round table, Hannah hung back until John sat down, then grabbed the chair next to him. Megan sat on the other side of him, and I sat in the chair opposite him, relieved to stay out of the fray.

The waiter distributed menus while other staff skittered back and forth, bringing us our drinks, our belongings, bread, and laying our napkins properly in our laps.

The waiter said he would give us a moment to look at the menus, then turned away, but John stopped him, and put a hand on my arm. "Lauren, you don't have a drink, what would you like?"

"Oh, a martini would be great."

"Yes, madam. Would you like gin or vodka?"

"Uh, gin."

"Any particular brand?"

"I like a very botanical gin with just a hint of vermouth."

"Just a hint...so very dry, dry, perfect or wet?"

"Wet." Wait, is that right? What is "perfect"? For that matter, what is "wet"?

"Shaken or stirred?"

Megan sighed loudly. John smiled.

I had no idea which to order. I could not remember how the bartender at the restaurant made it. "Uh, whatever."

"I recommend stirred."

"Stirred is great."

"And olives or a twist?"

"Can I get an onion?"

"I am sure that will be fine. Thank you, madam." He bowed himself away from the table.

My face reddened with the realization that something about my drink order was off, but I was not exactly sure what.

"Jeezus," Megan said. "Your drink takes as much time to order as food." This, from the queen of substitutions.

"Everything looks so good..." Hannah purred, studying the menu. "But so expensive. What are you going to have, John?"

"I'm going to have the Alaska salmon, but get whatever you want. This is my treat."

Hannah smiled at him, and Megan mumbled something about the prime rib, but he was already turning back to the table and me.

"So, what do you do, Lauren?" John said.

I assumed this was part of the introductions I had missed. "I work with Megan. At the same company, I mean, not the same job."

Hannah piped up with an oddly timed, "I work in H.R. I'm the floor representative."

John nodded at Hannah, then turned back to me. "Are you also in H.R.?"

Apparently, this had not already been covered.

"No, I work in Human Factors. I mean, my department works with them."

"Human Factors, so the interfaces?"

"Yeah."

"That's an important area." John leaned back and tapped his fingers on the table rhythmically. "Do you like it?"

"It's interesting. I mean, my department doesn't do the actual engineering, we mostly just write the documentation and help with paperwork."

"More interesting than logistics," Megan grumbled.

I knew Megan was not happy in her job, and I welcomed the chance to direct the conversation away from me. "What about transferring to another department?" I asked her. "Have you looked at the job postings?"

"Yeah...." Megan pushed the ice cubes in her cocktail around with her two mini-straws. "Most of them want a degree. Or make less money."

"So why don't you get a degree?" John said. "I'm sure your company will help pay for it."

Hannah piled on. "Yeah, they will."

Megan had been stabbing at the top ice cube in her glass, and now she threw the straws on the table with a sigh. "Because I don't want to."

"Do you have a degree, Lauren?" John asked.

"Yes."

"What is it in?"

"Sociology."

John turned back to Megan. "See? Just major in something you enjoy. Most of the time it doesn't have to be in the area you work in, it just shows you did it."

"No one believes that anymore. If I'm going to learn everything on the job anyway, why do I have to waste my time and money getting a degree?"

John kept at Megan with the persistence only family can deliver. "It shows you can do it. I'm not that much older than you and I hire people all the time and—"

"I know I *can* do it, I just don't *want* to."

"*They* don't know you can do it. But when they see you have a degree, it sets you apart from other applicants."

"Look," Megan leaned forward in her seat. "It's not the fifties! The education system is broken and overpriced, and it doesn't have the same value in today's job market! I'm not doing it."

"I have an Associate's Degree," Hannah said.

Megan turned her venom on her. "Congratulations, you managed to waste your time, money, *and* not have a degree!"

Hannah looked at her lap. "I have a degree."

We all watched as the waiter brought my martini over and placed it in front of me with a bow, then asked the table, "Have you had enough time to look at the menu?"

"Yes!" I said, looking—again—to derail the conversation. "You, John?"

"I'm ready."

We all ordered, then succumbed to the waiter's suggestions for more starters and first courses than we needed or wanted. The waiter nodded and smiled, walking away with our entire food order stored firmly in his head, while I could not even remember what I had just heard Hannah order.

"What do you do?" I asked John, guarding from a return to the previous conversation and noting that Megan and Hannah had returned to—or rather, not stopped—sulking. I felt that getting John to talk about himself would be the easiest way to guarantee a flow of safe conversation.

"I'm the Hardware Development Lead for my company."

"Wow." I nodded, more to encourage John to keep talking than from any genuine interest in hearing about it. But he seemed happy to talk, and I was relieved at least someone was.

Then, the appetizers landed, so John and I turned our attention to the new arrivals. Megan and Hannah remained motionless and expressionless.

"Hannah," I said, taking a big bite from some sort of fritter that I could not remember ordering. "This is delicious! Try one!" And maybe it was, I did not really notice.

She pursed her lips and pushed a corner of her mouth up, briefly, to acknowledge my attempted engagement.

I sighed and turned back to John to carry us through. "So, you were saying?"

He gladly obliged, and I worked hard to keep my mind from drifting the same way I did during these conversations at work, by furrowing my brow, nodding, and smiling.

To my relief, the next course soon arrived. Megan and Hannah stared through the salads placed in front of them.

"This looks great!" I said to everyone and no-one, thinking how I did not need this hassle tonight.

John inhaled the scent of his steaming soup with a smile, either oblivious to or not too concerned with the unhappiness at the table.

I focused intently on eating my salad. Megan and Hannah pushed theirs around on their plates, then pushed the plates away. John was deep in the blow, sip, blow choreography of eating his soup and did not seem to notice. No one talked, and I was sure we each believed that was for a different reason.

John was nearing the end of his soup, and I wanted to head off any return to the prior strife. "So, John, you're from Denver?"

He beamed at my interest. I realized he might be taking my conversation prompts in the wrong way.

"Yes, both Megan and I are from there. I've bounced around a bit, but I've always lived out west. Have you ever been?"

"No, I haven't." I glanced at Megan, but she had disengaged.

"It's beautiful. You should visit." Then he added, "And the tech industry there is really growing."

I was searching for an answer when the waiter came to remove our dishes. He asked Megan and Hannah if there was anything wrong with their salads, and they both shook their heads no, but offered no additional reassurance.

That gave me a moment to form a response that would add some much-needed context to tonight. "Oh, nice, my boyfriend is also in the tech industry."

"Boyfriend?" John asked and looked at Megan. Megan snorted.

"Yes, I live with my boyfriend, Kyle. He works on the software side," I said, intentionally over-sharing.

"Ah." John sat back in his chair, checked the time, then stared at Megan through slitted eyes.

Megan erupted. "For how much longer, Lauren? Things don't seem to be going so well."

Hannah's mouth dropped.

"Things are fine," I said, coolly.

"Yeah, that's why you spent the other Saturday night out with me, so you didn't have to go home."

My cheeks blazed. I could not believe she said it.

Hannah looked at both of us, hurt. "You didn't call me," she said quietly.

Then the waiter was back with his team, placing plates of food in front of us, asking if there is anything else he could bring us.

John quickly pulled out his wallet and handed over a credit card. "No, thank you, I'll just give you this now."

"Would you like me to run it, sir?"

"That would be great." John leaned back in his chair and looked around the room, avoiding our table.

And we were quite the table: John getting ready to bolt, Megan glaring at everyone, Hannah staring through her food again, and me. No one touched the food.

I turned to Hannah and put my hand on her arm. "I'm sorry, Hannah, it wasn't planned."

Hannah looked at me with large doe eyes. "But you didn't call me."

I did not know how to respond, and she looked down again. Then she stood up. "I'm sorry, John. I'm going to go. Thank you, it was nice to meet you."

John gave her a perfunctory nod and wave, and looked away again as she left.

The waiter returned with John's credit card and noted Hannah's departure.

"Is everything okay, sir?"

"It's fine. Thank you," John said as he scribbled his signature on the check. That done, he pushed back from the table. "Megan, Lauren." He gave us each a nod and walked out.

I leaned back in my chair, exhaled, and watched him go. Then I looked at Megan. She raised an eyebrow and took a long drink from her cocktail before picking up her silverware and starting to eat.

I stood up, slowly, and looked at her for a second before I headed toward the door, leaving Megan to her meal.

The next day at work, Hannah was quietly missing. I not-so-casually mentioned it to the woman who worked in the cubicle next to her whose name I could never remember.

"I saw her here this morning," the woman reported, swiveling her head, as if I had not already covered that level of searching.

The woman on the other side of Hannah's cubicle popped her head up, a good reminder that there was no such thing as a private conversation in the worknasium. "I think she's working on a project on another floor, or in a training, or something."

"Okay, thanks," I said. I turned back toward the path that led to my desk and caught Megan glancing in my direction from across cubicle-land.

"Do you want me to tell her you're looking for her?" said the forever-to-be-nameless woman.

I thought for a minute. "No, thanks."

I went back to my cubicle and flumped into my chair. I looked at the lifeless phone lying on my desk; my mom had not called or texted in more than a week.

I picked up my phone and typed, *Sorry haven't called. Busy with everything. Will call next week.*

Or the week after that.

An immediate response: *Okay. I love you.*

In the days and weeks following the disastrous dinner, Hannah, Megan and I all kept to ourselves at work. I smiled at Hannah when I saw her in the break room, and she returned the weakest and briefest of smiles, but then quickly left. I never heard that anything was being said about why we were not hanging out any more, but I was not sure if that was because nothing was being said, or because nothing was being said to me.

I still had not called my mom. I wanted to, but I did not know how to tell her what led up to the current state of affairs. Or I did not want to. Either way, I felt adrift, but knew I was the one who had cut the rope that had kept me moored.

Work became just work, without any of the intrigue or ill-advised drinking lunches. I tagged along on a couple of other co-worker lunches, but found them, and the co-workers, unmemorable.

I had been pushing Kyle to rejoin our circle of friends since the night at Reiser's—with very little success. I did not want to hang out with them by myself, afraid of what would be said about me and about Kyle, but I needed more than the gym to look forward to every day.

I had felt in-and-out-of-sorts since running into Ryan, but his comment about Kyle beating him at disc golf inspired me to push our friends to meet up for a round on some random Saturday that worked for everyone a few weeks later.

It could not happen soon enough for me: watching Kyle play disc golf was a thing of power and beauty. It was what first caught my attention about him.

Back then, I had been hanging out with Emma quite a bit, and I had met Kyle, who seemed interested in me, but I had not taken his interest to heart.

I winced to remember that Gabe had been the one I had originally noticed, because just based on appearance, he was definitely worth noticing. But ten minutes of talking to him had convinced me that "from afar" was the best way to appreciate Gabe. His undeniable good looks and athletic ability growing up had given him a confidence normally reserved for those who went on to add to those accomplishments. But Gabe had not. His lack of doubt about everything he did, said, or thought, despite what seemed like glaring deficiencies, was amazing to me. Emma told me that the only football scholarship offers he had received after high school were from small schools he considered unworthy of his skills, so he had decided to skip college and take a job as a technician at a local chain of oil change drive-thrus. It must have been a pretty good job for a high school graduate, but nine years later he was still there, technicianing, and not in an accomplished way. For some reason, the pride that had kicked in when making decisions about college seemed to have packed up and left him stranded. So, with Gabe a dead end, I had found myself window-shopping again.

Then, Emma had invited me to disc golf.

"But I don't play," I said.

"That's going to be a problem. I require my friends to maintain a top-twenty or better ranking in the Disc Golf Association of America."

"Is that really a thing?"

"Probably," she shrugged.

"So does that mean you cannot have more than twenty friends?"

"Only twenty I will hang out with. I have more, but they are usually jostling to get in the top twenty so they can see me."

"Of course."

"But no, I don't play either. A bunch of us stay and tailgate while those who want to play, play. It's a lot of fun."

So, I went. There were people I knew and people I did not, and there was Kyle. He was messing around with a couple of his friends before the round, throwing a regular frisbee in a game that turned into "tackle frisbee." It was there, watching him laugh and throw and run and wrestle with his friends, that I had decided to give Kyle a closer look.

When the players started off, I had tagged along to spectate. Kyle noticed right away, and maybe he was trying to show his plumage, but watching him dominate that day was what led to us going out the next weekend.

I needed to be reminded of that attraction I felt. Plus, I was not as dominant at anything myself, so it would give me the rare opportunity to talk reams of smack and actually have it backed up, which was always a plus for a girl like me who delights in smack talk.

It was just what I needed.

So the Thursday before disc golf, when Kyle said now he wasn't sure he wanted to go, my outrage was not just that of someone starved of outings, it was of a woman starved of inner excitement, as well.

"No! Everyone is already planning on being there! And you said you would go!"

"I'm just not sure I'm up for it. And it's going to be hot. They can play without us."

"But it was my idea!" I bared my soul, my teeth, and my breasts in an all-hands appeal to any part of him that was undecided on the matter.

Eventually, he relented, though I suspected it had nothing to do with my appeals.

We would be there, but once again, I felt like in order to live our life I was smashing myself against an immovable block of clay, one that was built to resist me, but only in the most passive manner possible. And no matter how much force I could muster, the best I could hope for was to malform it in the shallowest way around me.

That Saturday, a huge group of our friends, and friends of friends, gathered in the greenway for disc golf under a sun that promised unseasonable brutality. We were ready for beer already.

I saw people I had not seen in quite a while. Some of them seemed surprised to see us, or maybe I was just looking for that reaction.

"Lauren! Kyle!" I heard people calling to us. Kyle moved easily through our friends, smiling, pounding backs, and slapping hands. This was Kyle in his element.

I laughed to see Kaia there with yet another new guy.

"Lauren!" She grabbed my hand and guided me over. "It is so good to see you! This is Zach." Zach, like all of Kaia's guys, was handsome.

"Nice to meet you. Are you playing today?"

"I thought I'd give it a try."

Kaia laughed. "Give it a try!" Then she turned to me. "He's really good."

Zach laughed graciously, and I smiled. If Zach had been one of our regular group, this would have been my cue to scoff and tell him Kyle would settle it with him on the course, but since he was in the probationary phase, I let the opportunity pass. "I can't wait to see!" Yes, we would see, Zach.

I said my goodbyes and turned to walk away, but then I stopped and leaned in, discreetly, toward Kaia. "I saw Ryan a few weeks ago."

"Ryan! How did he look?" Kaia said.

"Really good."

Kaia smiled. "Hmm."

I laughed and picked my way through the group to where Kyle was standing with two other guys. I said my hellos and then my goodbyes, as they said they were about to get started.

I planned to follow him through the course when they started the round, as I usually did, but the non-playing hordes of friends urged me to stay with them for a little tailgating, protesting that they had not seen me for so long.

"When we get back," I promised. I heard a chorus of objections in response. Emma and Kelsey walked over to me and each grabbed one of my arms. "Come on, we brought chairs and drinks," Emma said.

I wanted to bird-dog the players, not loiter in the parking lot with the hangers-on, but the group was more powerful, if not in persuasion, then in the grip of their hands on my arm as I again tried to sneak away.

"Oh no no no!" Emma said, dragging me with her. I had never seen her act like this.

They had set up seven or eight camp chairs under a tree, and more people were sprinkled around sitting on the grass. A cooler full of iced drinks was open in the middle of everyone. Kelsey and Emma walked me up to a line of chairs and sat the three of us down as if we were about to speak on a panel. It was from this position I sullenly watched the players, and some spectators, head out down the disc golf course without me.

We all hooted and applauded as the players set off, but almost instantly the smiles of the group seemed to melt into something more personal. More invasive. Needles of apprehension raced through my veins.

"So, are you okay? What happened with Kyle?" asked Kelsey, already opening what was at least her second drink.

"What did you do when you found him?" asked Emma, sipping at her beer while shaking her head.

Everyone looked at me, waiting for the goods. It was awkward, unanticipated, and not what I wanted at all. I squirmed in my seat, nauseous from the unwelcome memories. I did not want to give the crowd a speech on "What happened to Kyle." I did not know what happened. I could not tell them. These were supposed to be my friends but their cued-up sympathy rang hollow. I could not handle the insincerity of it all.

"Oh, I don't know..." I said, looking away.

For the first time, I noticed Ann, sitting cross-legged on the grass a little apart at the edge of the group, her head bowed. Ann had always seemed to have the power of invisibility, or maybe she just wanted it. She sat there, sober and silent, as always. But of all the people I would have expected to be part of this inquisition, I would never have guessed her. Then, as if I had shouted this at her, she glanced up at me, quickly rose, and walked into the trees.

I looked after her; apparently I was the only person to notice her leave. Meanwhile Kelsey continued to prod me. "Did you know?"

The hair on the back of my neck stood up with an uncomfortable electricity. "No," I snapped at her, "Of course not."

Kelsey and the others persisted. It was clear the questions would continue until some satisfaction was had. But I held out. Eventually, I could see Kyle and the others gathering to play the final hole. After what felt like seven lifetimes, the winner of the round paraded over from the final hole. But it was not Kyle. I was satisfied to see it was not Zach, either. It was Gabe.

I looked for my hero, but his return a short time later was subdued. The mark around his neck that had been fading now glowed red-hot, a combination of the exertion and the sun. Like a cattle brand, something everyone could see.

I practically ran to him. He threw an obligatory arm around me and looked down at me, breathing hard but smiling. I looked up at him, my head full of questions. What answer did I want? He was more tired than he typically was, but that was to be expected since most of his sports had been observational lately. But he lost at disc golf? To these guys?

"How did it go?" I said, floundering.

"Pretty good. I'm a little rusty. Some good players out there today."

Pretty good? I'm a little rusty? Was he really so nonchalant about this? I looked over and saw Ann near the parking lot with her head bowed, and Dani rubbing her arms trying to catch her downcast eyes.

I wanted to leave. Kyle wanted to leave, too. There was a game on he wanted to see.

That night on the couch in the relentless heat of our apartment, I rubbed his sore muscles while he relaxed in front of the television. But this was no selfless act; I wanted answers. I wanted to know this was what we had to go through to get back to how things were before, but that we would get there someday. I needed to know that.

I threw my leg over him and sat on his lap, facing him and blocking the television. His first impulse was to keep moving his head sideways to see around me, but one firm massage to his groin let him know I would not be ignored.

He looked startled. I kind of startled myself as well with that move, but at least now he was looking at me.

I continued massaging, looking for answers, but he laid his hand on my wrist. "I'm really tired." I stopped, and withdrew my hand.

We looked at each other for one pregnant, unclear moment. I rolled off him, onto my feet, and walked without comment into our bedroom, to the edge of the bed where I felt like all my best lost time had been spent lately.

But when I looked up, I saw that tonight I had apparently chosen an edge visible from the couch, and that he was still looking at me.

I walked toward him, eyes locked, then reached out and batted the door to the bedroom shut.

I stared at this new barrier for a moment, then walked back to the bed and collapsed onto my back. I felt like the weight of everything pushing on me was too much to take in that position, so I grabbed a pillow and curled up to it in a stronger geometric form.

I pictured Kyle out on the couch. There were times I would just look at him without him knowing, or with him knowing but not caring. It did not matter which, the result was the same. Kyle sitting there. Kyle on the couch. Kyle being fed a constant diet of sports and flashing lights and men shouting. Since the hospital, he was like a smooth, glassy stone with none of the interesting pockets or protrusions he had had in our previous four years together. Now you knew him completely at first sight.

I thought about what I had just attempted. It was no use. That part of him was as damaged as everything else. He was sweet, gentle, almost simple, and it was maddening. I hated myself, and I hated him more. I felt like a river of hate flowing against itself.

We had become low, dull, pedestrian. The wit and vigor with which Kyle used to win at life had withered away, whether from the medications or the trauma, it did not matter.

But he did not choose this, I did.

He chose the quick death; I forced this slow one on him. When I found him I could have left. I could have waited to call 911. Are there take-backs? When I walked into our apartment that day and saw him, the logical part of my brain was never consulted. It was a pure base instinct to preserve life. But this life?

The stench in the room when I found him had been as inside-out as I felt; the response of his body to the violence of his task, I suppose. At the time, I was embarrassed for him. I tried to drag him free of it before the medics arrived, but there was no masking the smell. We all knew what had happened.

Now, the shadows in the bedroom started to stack up and I needed to escape the scene they were pressing into my head.

I opened the door and went to the kitchen to dig into what had morphed into our constantly stocked wine cabinet. Kyle looked at me but did not engage. Then he turned back to the television.

I went to grab the wine opener from the drawer and saw our checklist for the next week sitting out on the counter. Suddenly I saw it as a report on how things would be. As the appointments and sessions had dropped off, it had changed from being something to work on and turned into a description of our new life. Our. New. Life.

I pulled open the drawer of disappearance and pushed its contents around until I spied Ryan's card, lying there, waiting, partly obscured by to-go menus. Ryan knew. He knew, and was not going to pretend otherwise.

How did I not know? Who else knows?

My mom. She knows.

His mom. She must know. That is why she wants him to come home.

How many others know?

Megan? Was that what she meant when she said she did not know how I could still be with him? She was not talking about that incident or even that day. It was about the weeks, the months, and the unfolding of our new life. She was giving me a snapshot examination of what she saw as my previously stated, desired future and how that jibed with what she now saw. She knew.

Why had I not known?

Weeks and weeks passed before I can remember more.

I still had not called my mom, doling out only the briefest of occasional responses, and then only to put her off again.

I do remember that I had been avoiding certain people in our group, and big group events in general, to avoid a repeat of the disc golf incident.

Megan and Hannah and I had wordlessly moved into a new, neutral association, with smiles and acknowledgements and maybe a word or two, but nothing beyond that. Megan was fine moving on, and Hannah had started hanging out with a new, younger girl at work, which, for my part, made it easier to enjoy the relief that the death of those relationships brought.

Summer was sliding by.

One week, the city blazed with heat that no number of pulled-down-shades could thwart. It was hot—hot, heavy, and still. People think it is the night that is still, but really it is mid-day, when the heat is so stifling nothing has the strength to move and even the buildings seem limp in its onslaught. Days when it is too hot to enjoy coffee and instead you get something that emphasizes the strangeness of the day that has no morning coolness.

Kyle seemed fine returning home after work to sit, sweating, in front of the television, but between the heat and how crazed Kyle was making me, I was driven to spend more and more time at the air-conditioned gym.

Normally, I saw the gym as a means to enjoy the dinners and cocktails our friends regularly arranged and not look out of place among the beauties in our group. But that week I made it my religion and attacked it with the fervor of the newly converted. The results were negligible for anyone who was not seeing me naked, which right now was no one but me, but I still relished what I knew was happening under my clothes. I felt strong.

Coming home to the apartment after the gym was always an emotional passage for me. I did not want to go home. I did not want to see him. Or rather, I was not sure whether I wanted to see him until it happened, and then the answer was always no.

One night I crept, ever hopeful, through the doorway to see if that approach revealed anything different than the usual television blaring. No: television is blaring.

I deflated onto the entry bench and slipped off my shoes without untying them. I left them where they were and stared at them for a minute, wondering why they had chosen to bring me back here, before getting to my feet and walking into the bedroom to change out of my gym clothes.

Kyle turned to watch me walk by into the bedroom but did not say anything.

I walked out a minute later in my pajamas and went straight to the kitchen. I mixed myself a martini and gulped it down, then made myself another.

"You're sure drinking a lot lately." He said this from right behind me.

I jumped. I did not realize he would get off the couch without my prompting, but apparently diagnosing me with a drinking problem was a good enough reason.

"There's nothing else to do."

"Drinking is bad for you."

"Whatever. You used to drink, too, before you became King of the Couch. Besides, you think sitting in front of the TV all day, every day, makes you the picture of health?" My pointed look at his ever-increasing gut caused him to look down, but he said nothing.

I snorted derisively before turning away from him to paw through the day's mail. "At least you can play football this weekend instead of just watching it."

He said nothing. I looked up.

"The football game to kick off the preseason? That's this Saturday."

"Oh, I don't know...." He wandered back toward the couch.

I stopped and looked after him. No? To football? To the annual football game?

He dropped into the couch. "It's hot out, and there are some games I'd like to watch."

I continued to stare at him, unwilling to let him off that easy, but also not really caring what he did.

He turned to look at me, and his face turned red when he saw I was looking at him. "I don't want to go."

Still I stared.

He stood up from the couch, but it was not aggressive, more like a frustrated child. "I just don't want to go! I don't want to!"

"Okay," I said, emotions draining away.

He looked at me, still breathing hard and clearly in the throes of his emotions.

"Okay," I said again. At least we would avoid another incident like at disc golf.

I reached for a wine glass from the cupboard. "I'm going to read," I said, while filling my glass with almost one third of the bottle of wine I had opened the day before. I did not want to leave the bedroom tonight.

I walked to the bedroom with my outsized glass of wine and my martini, careful not to spill any precious drops. I could feel Kyle's frustration as I padded past him, but I did not care. I nudged the door shut with my foot, sealing my pod of solace.

The next day, I stayed longer than usual at the gym. And the day after that. It was an easy excuse to avoid going home. Besides, I was motivated by my recent gains, and I wanted to keep that momentum going. The admiring looks I was getting did not hurt either.

Kyle still had not been back to the gym, so it offered a bit of a refuge from that part of my life. Refuge, that is, until the perky front-desk girl with the perfect arms and flat stomach, Tish, stopped me on my way in Saturday morning.

"Hey, I called Kyle to ask why he had not been in lately and talk about how we could help keep him on track, but he said he was recovering from an accident? What happened? Is he okay?" She was standing there, as always, bright eyed and smiling, with arms akimbo like Supergirl just waiting for the wind to fill her cape.

"He's fine. Well, as he said, still recovering but..." I fake smiled and started to inch my way toward the entry turnstile again, only to be thwarted by Tish's vise-like grip on the topic.

"That's a relief! When he said *accident* I was so worried! Were you in the accident, too? What happened?"

A couple of people had walked in and paused to take in the conversation. "Who got in an accident?"

"Nothing really. He'll be back soon," I said, answering only the questions I wanted to, then pushing through into the gym and sitting down on the first machine I saw open. "Stupid calf machine." I grumbled. To my discomfort, I saw the people still hovering at the front desk to get the answers I had not provided.

I had already lost track of how many reps I had done in the faked exercise regimen I had initiated in order to escape Tish, and now I retreated to the always-abandoned stretching alcove to feign a preternatural focus on the stretching routine my sham workout apparently required. After a few minutes of nonchalance, I slipped out past the large exercise ball holding the side door open for airflow. It took an awkward, spread-eagle move, and I had to windmill my arms for balance after I caught the rubbery toe of my sneaker on the equally rubbery ball as I made my one-legged hop to freedom. I was sure the door led to a magical building foyer that exited on the opposite side of the building from the one shared by the gym, but as it turned out, no, of course it did not. It was a hallway that led to the same foyer as the one I had used to come in.

I peeked around the corner to see what an escape entailed. I could only see the edge of the front desk, so it looked like I'd have to endure an awkward walk out past Tish. But the final leg of the escape ended up being almost disappointing in its uneventfulness. No one was coming in or out. And it turned out Tish was not even at her post. Probably somewhere alerting more people about Kyle's "accident." I glowered.

Now outside the building in gym clothes and without a plan, I mulled my next move. It was early enough that the sun was still a welcome, warm glow on my skin, so I decided to take a brisk walk in a nearby park.

The park was beautiful, with a trail weaving its way around a small reservoir, through the mature trees and roaming waterfowl. In hindsight, it was a ridiculous plan to do on a beautiful Saturday when everyone would have the same idea. Most of my exercise that morning came from avoiding the melee of people not adhering to the drive right/walk right convention used in the U.S.

By the time I arrived home, I was hot under the collar in every way. Two of our friends had messaged, asking why we were not at the football game, but I was in no mood to respond, and I did not know how to answer that question anyway. Yes, why aren't we at the football game?

As I tromped up the stairs to our apartment, all I wanted was to see Kyle doing something, anything, besides wasting his day alone on the couch watching television.

I flung open the door to our apartment with a "Quick! Hide! My girlfriend is back!" startling Kyle who was sitting in front of the television watching sports, just as I knew he would be.

He turned to look at me, eyes big and confused. Of course, I thought, because his sense of humor is another thing that died that day. How fun for me.

I kicked off my shoes and ambled toward the kitchen for a glass of water. "I am funny!" I said, raising my arm in self-proclaimed triumph.

"Everything okay?" Kyle said.

I snorted as I pulled a water glass from the cabinet. "Oh. Yeah. Everything is great." I needed to stop. Or did I?

Kyle stared at me from the couch. I stared back at him. I filled up the glass from the tap, eyes still locked on Kyle. I guzzled the water, never looking away. "I'm going to take a shower," I said, in a manner that dared him to stop me, before stalking to the bedroom.

I took a quick shower, applied some makeup noncommittally, then grabbed the closest things from the top of the "almost clean" pile on the floor and threw them on.

I walked toward the front door once more.

Kyle leaned back to crane his neck at me in the entry hallway. "That was quick. Where are you going?"

I had not thought of that. My answer needed to be somewhere he would be sure to not want to go, like "away from the couch."

"Farmers market," I said, slipping into my shoes.

"What are you going to get there?"

"I don't know!" I flung open the door, passed through, and flung it closed again.

Once in the hallway, I knelt to tie my shoes, but realized I had forgotten my purse. I scowled at the locked door as if it had snatched my purse from me and now we would have to rumble. I sighed and hung my head. I set my jaw and bunched my fists. I could do this now or later, but I had to do it.

I knocked on the door. I heard shuffling, and the door opened.

"Lauren?" He seemed genuinely, annoyingly, surprised to see me. Good job, you are almost sure I am the woman you have dated for four years.

I leaned past him and plucked my purse from the bench, then turned and trotted away down the stairs. A moment later, I heard the apartment door close.

Bursting out of the front door of the building, I now had to decide what to do. I would have loved to go shopping, but my credit card balances were still uncomfortably high from Kyle's time in the hospital, so the farmers market it was.

I wandered in the direction of the market, noticing that the closer I got, the more the trickles of people joined to become rivulets, then streams, then a thick bustling flow, all headed toward what the farmers had to offer. We all jostled to be ahead of the others, even if we did not know our own ultimate goal, let alone theirs. We just knew we wanted ours first.

Once there, though, the flow split off into lazy puddles around the stalls, goals nearly forgotten. I meandered through, admiring the perfectly coiffed produce, thinking—though noncommittally—that I should learn to cook.

I noticed people's reusable bags and all the statements they made—I support public broadcasting, I do not eat meat, I eat meat but only meat that had a good life and death, I would rather be reading, I own a corgi dog. I wondered what social statement I made, wandering aimlessly with no bag at all—maybe: It's complicated.

Then there were the parents with children who were hot, cold, tired, hungry, thirsty, desirous, had to go to the bathroom, did not want to go to the bathroom, and sometimes all of them at once. Godspeed, I thought, shaking my head.

I thought about the last time I had been here, with Kyle. I remembered how badly that ended. I thought of all the damage that came from that day. Or really, from a day two-and-a-half months before that day.

That was over six months ago now.

Six months.

Something inside me warned me to not indulge in thinking about this. My feelings on the matter were a gloppy mess—one of those household catastrophes you try to clean with water, but that somehow causes it to become stickier, or hardened, or smellier, or whatever.

I thought of Kyle, not the one back in our apartment, growing moss and embracing nothingness. No, I thought of the Kyle that chased dreams and good times and, well, me.

Eventually, I tired of the candles and crowds at the market, and stalked off in a new direction, past block after block of row houses, head full of thoughts I did not want. Then I came to a smattering of small storefronts where a group of middle-schoolers slumped down the sidewalk with cold burritos and pizza, the one in front wearing a hoodie that read *Municipal Waste*.

I kept walking. The storefronts got bigger and newer, each block boasting another restaurant, the floors above them housing ever more potential customers. Things were happening here. The front window of a national retailer was in a public transition, with workers scurrying to change it from early summer's fashions to late summer's necessities.

The sidewalk became dense with people not looking at each other because their screens needed their attention, and not listening to each other because their ears were filled with music and podcasts and pundits. These were what the storefronts were up against. These were what I was up against, too. The feeling of not being seen or heard seemed more complete than ever, and I added it to the pile—the massive, shapeless pile—growing in the dark corners of my mind.

The last time I left the market I had called Megan and kicked off a regrettable series of events. There was no danger of that now with her, at least.

I walked and sulked until my hunger stopped contributing to my foul mood and instead overtook it as my primary motivator. I started eying the restaurants I was passing with actual intent, and stopped in front of one that had a line of people waiting out front. A line meant "good," right? What did they know that I did not? Through the window I could see a bar with two single seats open between the other couples there. I hated the idea of eating alone, exposed, out of place, not looking like anyone. But who would notice in this atmosphere? Only the ones I did not want to see me.

I approached the harried hostess who was directing the scene from behind a stand at the front door, and who gave me—at most—a quarter of her attention.

"Hi," I smiled. "Is the bar open seating?"

She did not even look up from her list before saying loudly, "There's no room at the bar." Then she looked up at me and behind me and paused, head tossed to the side with self-assurance rooted in a lifetime of security. "How many in your party?"

My cheeks flamed. "Just me."

"Oh." she said, not even trying mask her disdain, whichever of my potential vulnerabilities it was aimed at. I wished she would lower her voice. The groups and couples nearby all stared at us, the only entertainment that could be had in the moment. She shoved a menu at me and said, "Go ahead then."

I held my breath and looked at her for a second, undecided. Then, whether out of confusion or contempt, she arched an eyebrow and cocked her head, clearly unimpressed with me.

"Never mind," I said, and slipped away.

As I walked away, I could still hear her. "No idea! She said she wanted to sit at the bar, then she walked off when I said she could!"

I turned at the closest corner and exhaled, as if I had never learned object permanence as a baby and that scene no longer existed if I could not see it. As if I would waste that power on this situation if I had that ability.

My hunger had disappeared along with my confidence, so I walked again until my hunger, at least, returned. By now it was mid-afternoon and getting genuinely hot out. A movie, I thought: food, drink, air conditioning, and a dark cloak of invisibility. A quick search showed that the closest movie theater was one near our old apartment. I did not realize I had walked that far; or, was it not that far? I looked up and saw, rising above the trees, the cluster of shiny towers that used to be our neighborhood. I remembered how excited I was when Kyle and I first went to look at apartments in them, right downtown, and how I had felt so grown up signing that lease, more than any other. It cost so much we could not afford to get new furniture for it, but having our friends over, all of us taking turns drinking cocktails out on the small patio looking over the city, with Kyle's arm around me, made me feel like we were the "it" couple for one hot minute. I picked out the windows that had been ours and thought about the life, and death, that went on behind them—someone else's now.

I turned, forgetting about the movie, and headed toward home. I rewound my day, past the restaurants, the row homes, across the park where the farmers market was now being disassembled and packed into waiting vans, and up the stairs to the door of our apartment, where I stopped and rang the bell. There was muffled movement on the other side. Kyle opened the door and looked at me, confused.

"Did you forget your keys?" He stepped aside to let me in.

I reached in my pocket and dangled my keys as a silent answer.

He closed the door and watched as I peeled off my shoes and kicked them under the bench.

"What?" I said.

"I'm glad you're home. I didn't know if you were going to go out with Megan again."

"Nope. This is your chance to have a hot date tonight. Did you eat already?"

"No. What time is it?"

"It's time to eat. Do you want to order in?" I was already scrolling through menus.

"Okay."

"But we have to watch something besides sports."

"Okay."

"Okay." I looked at him, looking for that guy with his arm around me, and he looked back at me, looking for who knows what. I sighed and resumed my menu scrolling.

That night Kyle kept his word—technically—in that *we* did not watch sports, but that did not keep him from checking scores on his phone with the regularity of a train conductor.

Finally, I said, "I'm going to go read. Watch whatever you want."

Kyle picked up the remote and changed it to sports before I was even off the couch. I stared at him, full of resentment, wanting him to ask me to stay just so I could refuse.

I went to the bedroom and shut the door behind me a little more assertively than usual, trying to communicate my displeasure in a way that left everyone in agreement about my pleasurelessness.

I stayed up quite late that night in a home-stretch effort to finish my book, but Kyle did not come to bed before I fell asleep reading, still short of the end, and my place in the book lost, splattered on the covers.

The next morning, I saw Kyle was in bed next to me, though I had no idea when he had arrived. I slowly exited the bed and the bedroom with my book, determined to claim some quiet time before he got up.

I was spooning my coffee cup on the couch, trying to find where I had left off in my book the night before, when I heard him coming to life in the bedroom. I gulped down the last of my coffee and made for the bedroom as he headed for the coffee maker. By the time he was seated in his customary couch depression, I was out the door without a word.

I was not going to go to our gym again, but I was not going to stay home with Kyle, either. Stupid Kyle.

I strolled around our neighborhood, going into every open store. As it was before noon on a Sunday, there were not a lot of them. I walked past a small movie theater and, on a whim, decided to catch a movie, as I should have done the day before.

The first matinee was for kids, and though I could have waited fifteen minutes and gone to a grown-up movie, I opted for the earlier escape.

Inside it was a lovely venue, with red carpet and gold-painted trim, glamorous, if a little worn by its decades in service. The box office had just opened and I had a short wait before the movie started, so I picked up an obligatory box of popcorn from the snack bar and started looking for my theater.

I had my choice of seats. The aged springy velvet seats reclined to angles that varied from the ones next to them, and the one I chose groaned a brief objection when I sat in it.

I started in on the popcorn while the pre-movie ads were still rolling, counting them as part of my entertainment. I watched a few families find their seats, enjoying the tincture of chaos from children living their excitement about the forthcoming movie.

The kids continued to be an additional, free source of entertainment throughout the movie, laughing uproariously and shouting out things before they happened. They were either astute storytellers, or this was not the first time they had seen the movie. We all laughed and cried together until the end, and then we clapped.

I was reluctant to leave this happy scene and lingered until the last children were herded out of the auditorium, then I followed them out.

I emerged, blinking, into the light of day, and saw that I had missed another call from my mother. I lowered the phone back into my purse.

On the way home after the movie, I stopped to do the only quasi-real shopping I had to do, picking up an item I had not really run out of yet. Browsing my way through the rest of the aisles, I stayed long enough to realize the man I kept seeing aisle after aisle was probably security, and I had exceeded my browsing welcome period. Whether that was a brown person browsing welcome or a white person browsing welcome, I did not know. Perhaps those were both the same, though I doubted it. I felt like there should be a third category for a woman using the store to get a break from life.

While waiting in line to pay, I picked up a little plant that seemed to smile at me from a display at the front of the store, in the impulse section of the checkout area. I thought it would be perfect for my bedside table, and I welcomed the idea of another life in the bedroom besides me.

After the store, I walked, very slowly, toward our building. I thought of the time I ran into Ryan; I had not seen him since that day.

Eventually I could not help but arrive at our building. I walked even slower up the stairs until I was standing in front of our door. I could already hear the recorded clapping, whistles, and screams of the cheering sports crowd behind the door. I pretended it was for me, for a job well done, or just for showing the gumption needed to return home. I unlocked the door and pushed it open, setting my shopping bag down and letting the late afternoon sun that was streaming into the hallway envelop me as I raised my arms in triumph, much to the confusion of Kyle, who was still seated on the couch, watching the playoffs from three years ago.

I closed my eyes and kept my arms raised, needing every bit of support I could garner. They were cheering for me; I just knew it.

That is, until Kyle broke my spell. "Are you all right?"

I kept my eyes closed, but I dropped my arms as my bubble of illusion popped and fell to the floor as a moist film. I sighed, then opened my eyes and rid myself of my purse and shoes. "Yes."

Kyle was still looking at me. "I...uh..."

Yeah, I did not know would I would say to me either.

"I'm going to read." And I disappeared into the bedroom, again, for the rest of the night.

The next night, after work, I ducked into a dive bar that was closer to work than home, and disappeared into a creaky vinyl booth with a book. I briefly thought I should have called a friend, but then realized I did not know who that friend would be. Not because I did not have friends, but who among them should be saddled with all that came with this injured member of the herd?

After many chapters, and many cocktails, I dragged myself home.

When I arrived, I found Kyle had already eaten a dinner I had no appetite for anyway, and he was deeply absorbed in some game or another. As I stared at the back of his head, framed again in the glow of the television, I realized I had stopped being resentful that I was no longer an object of interest to him. I was not happy about it either; I just did not care.

I went to read my book in the peace of the bedroom.

On the third day after the gym incident, I poked my head into a different gym with no real intent, but only the justification that it was closer to our new apartment and I should at least take a look. It was nice. Not as nice as our other gym, but neither was there anyone loading me up with the baggage of being anything other than a lone woman looking at a gym near her new apartment. I joined. Sliding my credit card across the counter, I could feel the tension vacating my shoulders.

The next day, when I walked in, it was with a renewed sense of refuge, confirmed by the friendly front desk girl who would never ask me about an accident, a boyfriend, or the worst thing that had ever happened to me.

The next weekend, Kyle and I went to a work retreat for Kyle's company at a destination resort about forty-five minutes away. I was invited to play the role of "girlfriend/Lauren." It might not have been a critical part but for the fact that I had already been playing it for the past four years, and it would be odd if I was not there. (As if there was not a mountain of "odd" already sliding down around Kyle and me.)

We left Friday night and met up with some of his younger coworkers, still fresh with new-job excitement, in the bar of the hotel. I did not recognize any of them, but his was a big company, too, and people were always moving around to different projects, so I did not think much of it. I sipped my wine while they all talked work. More people joined, a few with spouses or partners, but overall, it was a pretty dull time for the plus-ones.

After the ironic "happy hour," the company hosted dinner in an expansive, low-ceilinged room below the main level that had none of the view or aesthetics of the public part of the hotel. It did not help that they had to keep the lights unmercifully bright so the staff could see as they carried food to and fro.

There was a short speech by someone high enough in the company that I knew nothing about him. He talked about planning for the future; I smirked ruefully. Kyle did not notice. At the end of the speech, the man closed by saying that the people in the room were the future and everyone clapped. Apparently clapping for themselves.

After the applause, the man sat down, replaced by the gradually increasing sound of clinking silverware and forced chitchat. I pushed some flavorless steamed vegetables around my plate, only vaguely aware of the heated discussion going on among the employees at the table (which was everyone but me) about what was the best platform for such-and-such. Kyle had always been the technology person in our relationship and kindly spared me the details. Things always worked, so I did not ask.

Dinner inched along through dessert, and finally I could excuse myself and go back to the room. I encouraged Kyle to stay and continue his fascinating conversation, and to my surprise and relief, he said he would, thanks.

I thought about stopping in the bar upstairs for a solo nightcap, but when I walked by it was full of people who had escaped from the same event. I did not want to generate questions from people who may have seen me at dinner, so I took my unexpected sanctuary in the room, instead opting for luxuriously low lights and its extra deep bathtub. It was a glorious thirty minutes or so until I heard the sounds of the door digitally approving entry, followed by Kyle saying, "Whoa, it's dark in here!" and all the lights flashing on.

I sighed and rolled my eyes as I listened to him walk around the tiny room asking repeatedly if I was there. I did not respond, knowing eventually I would be discovered.

Sure enough, almost immediately, because: tiny. Kyle popped his head in the doorway. "Oh, there you are. Did you hear me call you? Were you bathing in the dark?"

"No, I was bathing in the dim."

"Do you want me to turn the lights back off?"

I sighed again, breathing more air into the void between us. "No, I'm getting out anyway." I sat up with a slosh and reached for a towel.

His disembodied head disappeared from the doorway and I heard the television turn on, search around briefly, then settle on the sport du jour. Whatever it was, it was apparently better to look at than me. I stood up, toweled off, brushed my teeth, and slipped into my pajamas. It was eight-thirty.

I shambled out into the main room where Kyle was lying on the bed, fully clothed, absorbed in a game.

"Do you want to watch something together?" I asked.

"Okay," he said, clearly disappointed to share his screen.

"Never mind."

"No, we can..."

I grunted a negative. I did not care enough to fight over something I did not want with someone I did not want to spend time with. I opened the covers on the other side of the bed and crawled in, turning away from the lights, the television, and Kyle. I was pleased and surprised to feel myself relaxing into a deep sleep and welcomed the nothingness. I dwelt there, content, until late the next morning.

The next day, Saturday, Kyle had meetings during the day. He was already gone by the time I had formed enough resolve to throw back the blankets and involve myself in another day of my life.

I had scheduled a massage later that morning, and I planned to walk around the resort's gardens afterward, but that would not take a whole day, and I was getting tired of trying to find ways to fill empty hours.

I wandered down to the lobby where a coffee service had been set out and helped myself to a cup while I looked at all the pictures of the resort through the years, of its construction during the Depression, and its subsequent uninteresting use as a hotel.

I followed signs down to an empty workout area. I stepped onto one of the treadmills for a few minutes until I was concerned I would start sweating into my clothes. I hefted the dumbbells a couple of times, as if that would do any good, then walked down the hall to arrive early for my massage.

About fifteen minutes after I arrived at the spa, and five minutes after my massage should have started, a woman walked through the front door and walked briskly toward the back.

My masseuse, I bet.

Indeed, it was. Two minutes later, she was back, inviting me to my room and apologizing for her tardiness. And fifty-two minutes later she had wrapped it up and was escorting me out, ensuring she was on time for the next person.

I watched her bring the next person back and sighed. I headed back toward the front desk to ask about the gardens. I was cautiously optimistic when I saw a smiling woman behind the desk. Maybe she could be a turning point in my day.

"I read that you have some gardens? Which way should I go to see them?"

"We do! And they are beautiful! We have a full time gardener who lives on the property, and he does an amazing job. So if you see a man in a straw gardening hat, his name is Tom, and he would love to tell you about them." She pulled a map of the property out from behind the counter, circled a door, and leaned forward to point to a door down a side hall that corresponded with what she had circled. "You can start your garden tour at the end of that hallway."

"Thank you!"

"And if you enjoy that, you may enjoy the nature trail!" She leaned back and put an "X" on the map at the edge of the garden trail system. "It starts right here, and you can do a 1.5-mile loop, a 3-mile loop, or an 8-mile out-and-back hike to Lake Haskin."

"Thank you!"

"My pleasure! The paths are well-marked and the distances are on the signs, so it should be pretty straightforward, but don't hesitate to call us if you get turned around or tired, and we can come get you."

Turning point achieved. She even waved an excited goodbye, which is above and beyond in my book.

I did not see Tom the gardener, but she did not exaggerate the beauty of his work. The gardens were at once perfect and imperfect, in just the right way.

On my way around the garden, I realized I had arrived at the spot where the hiking trails started, and I decided to start my hike then, rather than finish looking around the garden.

The day had started to heat up and the forest ran a welcome interference play on the sun. When I set out, I had only planned to take the short loop, but the cool, flat trail beckoned me onward and I found myself walking past the signs marking the loops back to the hotel and heading for Lake Haskin.

I was not normally a hiker, but hiking this trail, I could see the attraction. Along the trail there were signs explaining the geology of the area, highlighting views, and pointing out some of the interesting flora, including several poisonous ones, which immediately made me itchy and, I thought, should have been the topic of the first sign.

After about an hour, the trees thinned out and the trail climbed slightly before undulating through rocky outcroppings. I was considering turning around, thinking how I still had another hour of hiking back to the hotel and that it was genuinely hot outside the shelter of the forest, when I topped a small ridge and the lake came into view ahead of me, blue and tranquil.

My phone signaled a message from Kyle. *Where are you? Getting massage?*

I looked at the phone, or at least in the general direction of the phone without really seeing it, for a long minute, then I switched over to *Do Not Disturb*.

I started down the trail toward the lake.

•

When I got back to the hotel a few hours later, Kyle, still in his business casual clothes, was already in the room watching television. Turning point concluded.

"There you are! I've been texting. Where did you go?"

I was kicking off my dusty shoes. "Sorry, I just got the texts. I found some trails in the woods. I think there was bad service up there."

"Oh." Kyle looked at me. I could not figure out what he was thinking. But then he looked back at the television. "We're supposed to meet some people in the bar before dinner."

"What time?"

He looked at the time, then back to the television. "In about forty minutes."

It was my turn to look at him for a minute. But I had nothing. I turned to get ready.

As promised, that evening we met up with people in his department for drinks before the dinner event. I joined with all the excitement of someone renewing her driver's license. Kyle chatted with work-related people I did not know about work-related things I did not understand. I filled the space next to Kyle.

Then one of his long-time co-workers, Charles, walked up and curled his arm around my shoulders, "Hey, Lauren, it's great to see you!" I was relieved to see him. I rewarded him with my most welcoming smile. He looked at me and frowned. "We never get to see you guys any more since Kyle moved to implementation."

Kyle moved to implementation? He had changed jobs? Was that a promotion?

"I know! And, you know, I have a new position at work that requires a lot of travel, too, so that is taking up a lot of my time."

"Oh wow, that's great. Well, I hope you get to go somewhere fun."

"You know how traveling for work is." Although of course I didn't even know myself. This was possibly the most adult conversation I had ever had, and I could not help wondering if I was out of my depth, but I did want to at least make an effort to keep up.

He stopped smiling and lowered his voice. "Hey, I'm sorry about what happened." What "happened," as if Kyle had tripped.

I nodded and looked at the floor.

"If you ever need anything..."

I nodded again, this time looking up, giving a weak smile. A lot of people had said that to me, and it always ended as an open question. I guess they did not know what I might need, either.

Charles gave my shoulder a squeeze, then walked away.

I turned my attention back to the man I apparently knew even less than I thought I did. I was ready to ask him about implementation as soon as his current conversation wrapped up, but as I stood listening to him for the first time that night, waiting for my moment, it occurred to me that his conversations were nothing more than a "best of" track that had been running out of him all night, nothing but a repeating loop of old observations, old comments, and old jokes.

His conversation broke up, but I could not move to inject myself before a new one gelled.

I listened intently for the next few minutes and realized I was overreacting, and Kyle was already on to a new topic. What was my problem? So what if he used a couple of old favorites? I listened to the new story, smiling just from the joy of the unfamiliarity, until one of his guffawing co-workers crashed through my storyline with the reality of, "Remember when you first said that to Raj in the quarterly meeting? Remember his face?"

My fears were realized. Everything he was saying, and all these laughs, were old material. They were things he had said a thousand times.

I stopped smiling and looked at him, trying to pack the scene into my head. I stared at him, tears threatening even in the midst of the crowd. As I stared, I willed him back to life: he looks like him, but he is not him. I wanted him back. I hated his simple smile and his simple calmness and his simple simplicity. I wanted to be mad at him for besting me in a game of wits instead of for being so boring. But boring was all he was anymore.

We went in to dinner accompanied by some of his new colleagues whose company ensured the minutes would drag like months. I barely talked, partly because I could not claw my way out of my own head, and partly because I had nothing to add to the technical conversation they seemed to never tire of. Kyle had not noticed and no one else tried to draw me out. It was only when the weary waitstaff started to take down tables that one of the masters of social cues at our table proposed moving to the bar. So I followed Kyle and two of his dateless colleagues over there for one more drink.

I could have happily downed a dozen drinks right then, but I had to maintain appearances—although at this point, God only knew why. I stared into the eddying brown liquid in my cocktail glass, a new drink for me, watching the ice melt into, and be overtaken by, its contents. I gave the glass a rough swirl, downed the rest of the drink, and told Kyle I would meet him back at the room. He turned to look at me, puzzled, but I was already walking away.

Back in the room, I lay on my side on the bed, still fully clothed, looking out the window into the night at the dark mass of trees I had walked through earlier that day. I noted that thankfully nothing on me itched, despite my earlier certainty that I must have walked through at least one, if not all three, of the poisonous plants in the area.

Only about five minutes passed before I heard Kyle at the door.

I heard his voice behind me but did not roll over toward him. "Hey, are you sleeping?"

"Not yet."

"Sorry, I just wanted to make sure you're okay. You left quickly."

"I'm just tired."

"Do you mind if I go back?"

"No." Go.

"Want me to turn off the lights?"

"No." Go.

"Okay, I'll be back in a little bit."

I said nothing, and a few seconds later I heard the door pull closed. Still, I stared out into the darkness.

The next morning we woke up, robotically packed, and headed home.

For many miles as I drove, I ran through every potential conversation I needed to have with Kyle until I settled on one.

"I heard you have a new job," I said.

"Uh-huh."

"You never mentioned it." I paused in case he wanted to mention it now, but hearing nothing, I continued. "When did that happen?"

"Beginning of May."

That was just a couple of weeks after he went back to work, and over three months ago now.

A few miles went by before I talked again. "Do you like it? What do you do?"

"It's fine. I just install the programs at the client site and make sure they work."

"So, troubleshooting?"

"Sort of. If something doesn't work, I try to get it to work, if it's a simple fix, but if it's not simple, I send it back to be fixed."

He can only do "simple" fixes? That sounded like a far cry from what he had been doing: programming on large projects, and even managing some small ones himself. I was mute.

"Do you mind if I watch a game while you're driving?"

Talking seemed impossibly difficult in that moment, so I just nodded my head.

"Is that okay?"

"Yes," I whispered.

He put in ear buds and stared at his phone.

I stared straight ahead, expressionless. I watched as the city skyline came into view and loomed closer and closer.

My days devolved into work, gym, bedroom. Repeat.

I avoided talking to our friends, and I recognized there was no great push on their side to cross that void either. Whatever. They had mostly started out as his friends anyway. But really? *None* of them were going to reach out? This was the group we had spent most of the last four years hanging out with! At least Kyle had an excuse.

My mom did keep calling me, but I never picked up. I could not explain it, but I just could not face talking to her. There was no rational explanation for it. She would be the loving, caring person I could talk to through this, the one who would have good advice that could help everyone in this impossible situation, but I just could not do it. So her calls and messages kept coming, and her concerned voicemails kept filling my inbox, and with each one I lowered myself deeper into the miserable hole I was digging for myself. *I love you, Mom...I'll see you on the other side of this*, I thought when her call appeared once again on my phone.

•

One industrious Saturday a couple of weeks later, when I had nothing else planned and Kyle could not be separated from his new mistress, sports television, I started cleaning our apartment with a wholesome fury. But I iced over when I reached the bottom of the mail pile to see the old recovery checklist. Some things checked, some things...not.

I started sobbing. Choked, helpless sobbing.

He turned on the couch so he could look at me, but it was like a chimpanzee trying to figure out a karaoke machine—total confusion about what inputs were causing the current outputs.

I screamed heartlessly at the chimp. "Why didn't you tell me? Why didn't you ask for help?" My voice broke seven different ways saying it out loud for the first time, and I was not even sure it had been intelligible. "Didn't you think *we* were worth staying alive for? That *I* was worth staying alive for?"

I rushed into the bedroom and locked the door for the first time ever. I sat in a trance on the edge of the bed. I could hear him try the door, knocking quietly a couple of times, but I could not respond. Like him that day so many months ago, everything inside me was on the floor, and I had nothing left to do anything with.

I curled up with a pillow, accepting the comfort it offered.

Getting back to the way things used to be was my goal, not his, and I felt monumentally stupid for not realizing it sooner. He had given the ultimate critique on our life.

And now...we were so far apart on how we felt about things. How could I not know? Why could I not help him? Worse, how could I try to pour him back into that mold again after...

I looked at the little plant on my side table that I had picked up in the store that day, pleased to see it thriving in the sun that had been making me suffer.

But I did not want to look at happy things right now.

I rolled over and looked at his side of the bed with its nearly barren side table, the dent of his head still in his pillow, the rays of sunshine from my side creating a shadowy monochromatic landscape.

Too much.

I sat up and swung my legs off the side of the bed, looking out the window at the untroubled people on the sidewalk not burdening themselves with these types of questions. Or maybe they were. Maybe another person would be in my position tomorrow.

I wished I could talk to them. Or maybe to the person in that position a year before me. Or ten years before me. Ann.

Maybe the doctor had played it perfectly, letting me check this realization off my checklist as I got here. No shortcuts.

It was too hard. I did not want to think about it and I did not want to deal with it anymore.

I turned around and looked again at the shadowland that held his body at night—and before all this, sometimes during the day. Sometimes for days at a time. There were those times when his jocularity dried up completely and he would fold in on himself with no opening to the world. Why hadn't I talked to him about that, found him some help?

Because I did not know. He was my first real boyfriend, so I did not know. I just feared. And even if I did know, it was too hard.

I gathered the comfort pillow in my lap. Massive torrents of tears streamed silently down my cheeks, slowly pooling, then shrinking into the pillow. I rolled up onto the bed again, still clutching the pillow.

I did not know.

I am so sorry, Kyle. I failed you.

My exhaustion formed a whirlpool that pulled me into a silent, black chasm of sleep that I did not emerge from until early the next morning. I robotically showered, dressed for the gym, and opened the bedroom door.

Kyle was asleep on the couch.

I looked at him for long minutes, then put my shoes on and left.

I bought a coffee on my way to the gym and stayed there for a couple of hours, though later I could not recall what I did there, or for the rest of that day.

The scene from the day before never came up again.

That night in bed I stared at the shadowy area next to me. I knew what was there: him on his side, exercising his right to breathe in, then out, then in, then out. Claiming each breath. He did so quietly, regularly, without fanfare. But he did it. Over and over, he did it.

I imagined him stopping. Again. Maybe I would let him.

Maybe I would let him.

•

At work the next day, I stared at the phone on my desk like it was my enemy. It rang. I jumped but took no other action. It rang again; the little screen let me know what was coming. I steeled myself and greeted the receiver. I swallowed hard and hunched over my keyboard, walling out the rest of the world.

"Yes, thanks for calling me back, Dr. Ehrlich."

Ten minutes later I hung up, staying frozen in that position as if removing my hand from the phone meant my turn was over and I could not take it back. Finally, I leaned back.

I stared at the notepad in front of me with its lists of .org web sites, and the names of people and groups for me to contact. For me. How had I suddenly become the patient? I guess I knew how: patients are people that can be helped. That was not Kyle anymore.

If I had been paying closer attention to what the doctor was asking in the beginning, in that emergency room, I would have understood how much we did not know—how long it had been before I had found him, how long his brain had been deprived of oxygen.

Dr. Ehrlich was a kind man, however, and today on the phone he had let me off the hook. He had assured me everyone's loved ones go into these situations with emotions high, thinking they will see the best possible outcome, and for the most part they are eased into the reality of the situation as time goes by, whatever that reality may be. I realized I, perhaps, had been a little more naïve than most. His mother knew, though. Definitely. Had she given me the time to get there on my own, too? Or was that giving her too much credit?

What happens now? Do I even care? Why do I have to deal with this when it was not even my problem in the first place?

I hated myself for thinking this. Still, I thought it.

"Lauren? Are you okay?" Jim had walked up behind me.

I swiveled to face him, still dazed. "Um...no." I looked at my lap again. "I think..." What did I think? What could I tell him about what I thought? "Um, that was Kyle's doctor."

He lowered his voice. "Your boyfriend?"

"Yeah."

"Is he okay?"

I paused. "No."

"He didn't—"

"No."

Jim waited for me to speak again.

"Can I take the rest of the day off? I just need some time..."

"Sure." Then he added, "Do you think you'll be out tomorrow, too? I could get Devon to jump on your project..."

"No, just today. I just need some time..."

"Why don't you head out. I'll see you tomorrow."

I nodded, slowly, but did not move for a minute. Then, in a flurry, I grabbed my purse and sweater and left. I saw Hannah peek over the top of her cubicle at me rushing toward the stairs, but she did not say anything. I jogged down the stairs and through the main foyer of the building and out the front door.

I started for my bus stop, but instead, continued up the block toward The Sidewinder. I pushed through the door into the privacy of the blackness inside, strode past the patrons at the bar, and sat in the corner.

The same bartender who waited on us before came over with a menu, which I waved off. "Just a gin and tonic, please."

He wandered away to make it happen.

I propped one elbow up on the table and repeatedly smoothed my hair back, unconscious I was doing so. I thought about what Dr. Ehrlich said, I thought about Kyle, and I winced when I thought about what our life together had turned into.

Then my drink appeared on the table, and I snapped back to reality just enough to thank the bartender for bringing it. I stirred my drink and took a long sip, wanting to change my frame of mind as quickly as possible.

I thought about our friends and what they would think.

I closed my eyes and returned to the comfort of playing with my hair. I finished my drink and motioned to the bartender for a second one.

A moment later, the second one appeared.

"I'll just pay you now," I said, grabbing my purse. I gave him cash, which I only had because a co-worker had paid me for a lunch order I put on my credit card, but which I was glad to get rid of. I quickly downed the second drink, took my glass up to the bar and set it on the counter, and left. Outside, the sun glared, as if trying to expose things I was trying to keep hidden.

I walked back to my bus stop and welcomed the feeling of the drinks making their way through my veins like a bore tide. The bus came in two or ten minutes, whichever, it did not matter, and I made my way to the back. There I sat, tense, barely aware of the world swirling around me.

When I thought to look up, I found we were only about two stops from the apartment, and I jumped to pull the cord. The bus braked, violently, at a stop we were just about to pass, and I lurched out the back door onto the street. I looked up and down the street and saw a restaurant I had been to a few times, and I knew it had a lounge on one side. I made my way there, thankful they opened early for lunch, and beelined for the bar.

I was the only one there, so I indulged myself by sitting in one of the booths at the back.

The bartender, an older woman with mounds of gray hair affixed to her head, followed me to my seat and set a napkin on the table. "What can I get you, hon?"

"A dry gin martini."

"Do you want a food menu?"

"No thank you."

"Be right up."

I went back inside my head again, trying to parse out something that had no separable parts. My martini arrived, and I sat there, cradling it, trying to see past the current fog into my future. True to its nature, the fog revealed nothing. I would have to step forward to see more.

I drank my martini, plus one more, then went home.

I laid on our bed, letting sleep and despair and alcohol control the afternoon.

•

That evening, when Kyle got home, I was pretending to myself that I still did not know how everything would play out. I looked at him sitting on the couch, absorbed in the television, watching sports highlights, and felt nothing.

"Maybe you should go home for a visit," I said with forced casualness, while flipping through the day's mail.

Kyle looked away from the television and straight at me. The part of me that had strategized this not-so-innocent plan thought: Wow, when is the last time I won that face-off for his attention?

"You just seemed so happy when they visited, and your mom really wanted you to come visit." I held my breath.

"Move home," he corrected, then his head turned to its natural resting place facing the television. "Yeah, maybe."

I looked at the back three-quarter view of his head for a long time, reviewing the tape of recent events and wondering whether the decision on the field would stand.

In the days that followed, where I needed to—but could not—extricate myself from my life with Kyle, I instead flung myself headlong into my days of work, gym, bedroom, repeat.

My work provided a haven. I realized I was getting a lot of satisfaction out of it, and more work gave me more satisfaction. My boss, Jim, noticed the renewed, or in all fairness, *new* commitment to my work and singled me out for praise in that week's group meeting. I blushed and smiled when the other people in the group nodded and clapped. It was the happiest I had felt in months.

"Did you talk to your mom?" I asked Kyle the following week. It was a test. He could fight for me still. And though it would do no good, I desperately and selfishly wanted him to. And not to. What was wrong with me?

"No."

Work, gym, bedroom, repeat.

Work, gym, bedroom, repeat.

"Did you talk to your mom yet?" It had been weeks. Now I just wanted some resolution.

"Yes. She bought me an open ticket."

Well, there it was.

I was stunned, though I did not know why.

I folded up next to him on the couch, curling my legs up in the way that had always let me feel small and protected next to him. Against my wishes, my eyes filled to the breaking point with emotion. He looked at me like I was a curiosity in a sideshow, but did not move to reassure me.

He continued, "I already gave notice at work. I thought I'd leave Saturday. Dad will be off work, so he can pick me up then."

How practical. And he already gave notice? I said nothing and looked out the window, swallowing what was lurking in my throat and ready to betray me. Saturday was two days away.

"I can help you with rent for the next few months, until the lease is up here and you find a new place." I wanted with all my heart to say I did not need his help, but the truth is I did.

Then he turned back to the television, and any emotion I had about the matter dried up instantly. I remained there for a minute, then uncurled and went to take a shower.

I woke up—or think I did, if I had fallen asleep at all—the next morning, alone in the bed. I opened the bedroom door and looked out. Kyle was asleep on the couch. I gently closed it again and got ready for work.

Twenty minutes later, dressed and ready to go, I looked out again and Kyle was still asleep. I padded softly to the kitchen to get coffee, and suddenly realized the machine belonged to Kyle. Was he taking it? He was going home; he did not need it, right?

I looked around at the kitchen, then the living room. It was the first time I had thought about us as separate entities, and about what parts we were entitled to from our shared life.

I went through the motions of working that day, although all I could think about was what my life would look like after Saturday. Tomorrow. Saturday is tomorrow. What would I tell our friends? *He* was leaving *me*, right? I *tried*. It is not my fault!

I skipped the gym that day and went straight home after work.

Opening the door, I could see the difference in our apartment. Parts of it were missing. Only my coats hung by the door, above only my shoes lined up by the wall. Even Kyle was missing from the scene, missing from his customary position on the couch. But everything else was still there—coffee maker, stereo, television, couch, everything.

I walked into the bedroom and he was there, stuffing stacks of clothes from the bed into a large hockey-style bag. His new paunch pushed his shirt out every time he bent over.

He stopped packing when I walked in. "Hey."

"Hi." We looked at each other. The lump in my throat was back. I looked down at his bag to hide anything that may have been showing on my face. "Will you be able to get everything in there?"

He looked at the bag and pulled up the sides, as if that action could create more room. "Yeah, I think so. I took a bunch of my stuff down and donated it, so I should be able to get the rest in."

I nodded, permitting a half-smile only so my quivering lip did not give me away.

He looked at me again. "I'm just leaving everything else for you. I'm sorry I'm leaving you with the couch."

Now my chin quivered at the thought that I had been worried about that this morning. Was I a bad human being? I looked away to the other side of the room so he could not see my emotional tumult.

I noticed the shadows stretched across the room in a new, autumnal way—longer and weaker than before. The little plant on my side table did not seem to smile as brightly, either.

"I don't think that plant is getting enough sun in here. Maybe I'll move it out to the living room."

Kyle looked at it and nodded, then went back to packing.

I went out to the living room with the little plant and stood there, as if deciding where it should go was the most important issue I could resolve right then. Maybe it was. I set it next to a window and stepped back to judge how happy a plant like it could be in a place like that.

I was still standing there when Kyle came out of the bedroom, toting the oversized bag.

"I think that does it."

I turned to face him, with way too much to say and no way to say it.

"Are you, uh...are you going out tonight?" he said.

It had not occurred to me what to do tonight. Do we go to our opposite corners and take uneasy glances at each other all night?

"Yeah. I'll probably be home late." Should I still call it home when it is only my home now?

"I'm just going to stay in. My plane leaves kind of early."

"Oh, well, I'll drive you."

"If you want. That would be nice."

"Okay, yeah."

"Okay."

We looked at each other and my cheeks flamed. I was flustered at how quickly this plan had developed, and I looked around for my purse. "Ummm, yeah." I found it on the bench, where it always was, and fumbled to add my keys and phone to its contents, then walked back out the door. "Bye."

"Bye."

I started walking down the stairs, double-checking I had everything with me, and wondering what I would do that night. I should call my mom, I thought, though I knew I could not. Not yet.

Many hours later, after I had digested most of a new book I bought, along with a lot of decaf diner coffee and some pie, I stood on the sidewalk outside our building and looked up at our dark apartment windows. I walked up the stairs, quietly turned the lock on our apartment door, and stepped inside. Kyle was asleep on the couch again.

Was I disappointed or relieved he was not in our bed? I did not want to answer that. It was stirring up feelings I did not want to deal with. He was leaving tomorrow, and that was how this was going to end.

I crept over and looked down at him. It is so confusing to see someone you love replaced by someone you do not, but the face of the one you love is still there, looking at you, breathing next to you, knowing you.

Tears again.

I turned and went to the bedroom.

Saturday came.

I rummaged through the kitchen drawer for the key to my car. We crammed his bag in the back and the two of us in the front, and I headed toward the airport. My job was to get us there, and it made it easier to not think about what was happening.

His mom was probably excited to have him back and to know her poor assessment of me was right all that time, I thought bitterly. No one will be bugging him to go out all the time and he can just watch television all day, and marry some white girl from his hometown. Just like Helene always wanted.

I glanced at him while pretending to check traffic and quietly snorted my disdain at the complete lack of emotion on his face. He could not care less.

As we approached the airport, I moved into the lanes for parking, not departures. Kyle said nothing.

I parked and opened the back of the car so Kyle could swing the swollen bag onto his back. I followed him into the terminal and watched, silently, as he checked in and handed his bag over. Then we made our way over to the security entrance to his airline's gates, and he looked at me intensely for what I realized was the first time in a long time. "I'm sorry for everything."

"For *everything*?" I teased, blinking away the tears.

"Not everything." He smiled at me, for real this time, a bit crooked with a hint of mischief. There was a glimpse of the man who won my heart, in spite of myself. But just a glimpse. Girl, let it go. Hold it together.

Kyle hugged me with one arm even while he looked down the hallway he would never return through. He was already gone. How many times had I thought that?

He joined the queue filtering through the checkpoint. Not only did he not look back, I know it never even occurred to him. I stared down the hallway long after he had disappeared to the other side. What was I hoping to see?

I walked back to the parking garage as tightly wound as a tourniquet, holding back floodgates of I'm-not-sure-what. In my car, I sat—stiff-armed—bracing myself against the steering wheel, staring.

Then I screamed. Loud. I yanked at the steering wheel. I flailed. And when I stopped, breathless, hair spiderwebbed across my face, registering the shock of the people walking by, I did not care.

I jammed the car into reverse and pulled out, a little too fast, and then threw it into drive and pulled away, a lot too fast.

Out on the main road, I thought, again, about that day so many months ago. It occurred to me I never asked Kyle if he was glad I saved him. "Saved him"—was that the right way to say it? I had never asked him why he had done it. And now he was gone, with the answers to both.

A car behind me honked, and I realized I had slowed to a crawl and traffic was stacking up behind me. I waved an apology and moved over to the slower lane and nudged the gas.

That night I hung out with some of the group. I had finally reached out to them because sitting alone in the apartment felt unendurable, even though, really, I had been alone there for months.

That evening's plans started out as a girls' consolation night out and grew into nearly all the old gang in various states of inebriation. And Ann, the one person who may have been able to provide that consolation, was unaccountably missing. But for all the drinks as I had, I felt nothing. I was a monolith, raised to some as-yet-undiscovered purpose.

The group cloistered around me, risking time with me, the weakest gazelle, injured by association. I looked at the herd, and its façade of undiminished confidence. But was it? They struck me as unsure, twitchy. There was no comfort for them in being reminded the next sick or injured gazelle could be one of them.

As the night wore on and the drinks continued to flow, the congress of our friends opened the floor to a general discussion of the recent events of my life, and I was thankful for the passivity my newly-stony heart allowed.

I told them a little bit. What did it matter now? What I knew had not given me any answers, but maybe it would help them.

But it did not, not really.

Eventually, the herd bored of the subject, clearly somewhat disappointed that my presence had not added much to the discussion. Someone suggested we move to a new venue. The group rallied behind the idea, and I watched with amusement as the bartender was besieged by, well, *everyone* trying to close their tab so as not to be left behind in getting to the next place. I stood patiently, as monoliths do. Waiting. Dissolving into the shadows.

As everyone filtered out, some did not notice I had not moved to follow them. Others noticed, but seemed fine to carry on without me when I said I was tired and going to head home.

I saw our friends Sara and Alexander, who had moved Kyle and me out of our old apartment, waiting for their turn with the bartender. I reached for Sara's arm. She turned toward me and smiled broadly, giving me the lightest of hugs. Alexander turned around too, and rubbed my arm warmly. "Hey!" they both said.

"Hey," I parroted back, shouting over the din. "So I always wondered...what did you do with the things...that didn't make it to the new apartment?"

They exchanged uncomfortable looks and she lightly hugged me again. "Oh honey, we just threw those out. We didn't think you would want them."

"No! No, we...I...definitely did not want them." I paused for breath. "Thank you, again, for taking care of all that."

She gave me one more light hug and they moved to the other side of the bar, ostensibly to finish cashing out.

I was still standing there, feeling a bit tender, when Kelsey lurched up to me, holding a cocktail she clearly did not need. I had not seen her, purposely, since she had strained my already-limited affection for her that day at disc golf. She supported herself on my arm, spilling out some slurry consolation, then she added, "You're better off! He is pretty dull now. And we don't have to feel guilty about not wanting to hang out with him!"

I stared at her. She was too busy looking around to notice.

"Okay," she declared, then wobbled out the door on her too-high heels to grab the arm of Brock, who was outside talking to Gabe. Brock looked down at her practically sliding down his arm and laughed, and I knew I should try to do the same.

"Ignore her." Isaac had walked up to me, giving my hand a reassuring squeeze. "I'm sorry about Kyle. Are you going to be okay?"

I looked down and thought about the question— Would I be okay? I lifted my head. "Yes."

Isaac smiled. "Don't disappear again, okay?"

"Okay."

"Okay. Are you coming with us?"

I looked around at the fast-emptying bar, then back at Isaac. "No."

He nodded, paused, then nodded again, and moved toward the door.

I do not remember much after that. The group was mostly gone, except for a couple of people locked in conversation. I felt relieved to be forgotten.

I nursed my drink until the last stragglers realized the herd had moved on, and that they needed to chase it to the next green grassland. After those last few hasty goodbyes, I moved to be by myself at the bar and ordered one more drink. I did not know it then, but it would be one of the last drinks I would have.

In a bar full of people, I appreciated sitting there quietly, in my own head, where no one else could go. I told myself that I liked being there.

I thought of him. Kyle. The old him. The real him. I hoped he felt better now.

I needed to call my mom.

About the Author

Bristol was born in Alaska, and named after Bristol Bay, where her parents fished commercially. Later, she was raised in South Central Alaska, splitting time between her family's off-the-grid homestead at Flat Horn Lake, and attending school in Anchorage. She now lives in Portland, Oregon, with her husband, dog, and way too many books.

About Tortoise Books

Slow and steady wins in the end, even in publishing. Tortoise Books is dedicated to finding and promoting quality authors who haven't yet found a niche in the marketplace—writers producing memorable and engaging works that will stand the test of time.

Learn more at www.tortoisebooks.com or follow us on Twitter (assuming the website still exists when you're reading this) @TortoiseBooks.